A RETURN TO FAITH

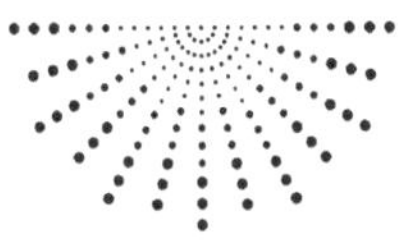

SARAH MILLER

SWEETBOOKHUB.COM

If you love Amish Romance and the sweet clean stories of Sarah Miller, you can join her for the latest news on upcoming books http://eepurl.com/bdEdSn

Your information will never be shared and will only be used for new release announcements, special offers on books, and exclusive previews and content.

Sarah Miller can also be contacted on Facebook https://www.facebook.com/SarahMillerBooks
She loves all things about the Amish life and would love to hear from you.

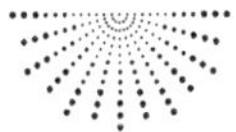

* * *

"I have told you these things,
so that in me you may have peace.
In this world you will have trouble.
But take heart!
I have overcome the world."
- John 16:3

* * *

A COOL BREEZE lifted the ties of her bonnet and let them fall gently against her neck. Roseanna Wagler brushed the tie away absently and closed her eyes. The breeze felt good and clean with the scent of grass as she moved through the field. It eased the weight from her shoulders and cooled the sweat on her brow. Today was a perfect day to be working in the meadow. The sort of day she lived for and there was plenty of work to be done.

Opening her eyes, she glanced across the land. How she loved this view. The vista of green spread out before her like *Gott's* perfect patchwork. There were fields of grass, dotted with black and white Friesian cattle. As she watched, she could almost smell their earthy scent and hear their moos as they came in for milking.

Her eyes moved across to the horses, bays, the occasional gray, and the big chestnut Dutch horses that the landscape and the Amish were famous for. Then there were the beautiful mixed colors of corn spread out before her along with all varieties of potatoes, vegetables, and the river in the distance. It was perfect, peaceful, and filled her with joy and only a touch of loneliness.

Wiggling her bare toes in the earth she lowered her head and looked at their own fields. It was good fertile soil and the crop would be heavy this year. The barley was not quite turning. The ears were still upright and the color still green. As it ripened the nutty scent would increase, but for now, it was sweet and barely detectable. This was the ideal time to walk between the rows to pluck out the weeds. So why was she feeling guilty?

The sound of hooves traveling on gravel carried across the field and her eyes were drawn to the buggy. The horse was trotting fast. It looked like *Daed* was worried. Maybe she should have gone with them. Roseanna's hand reached down and wrapped around the wild oats. With a quick pull, she ripped out the weed and placed it in her basket while walking along the row without needing to look. Up ahead a large patch of weeds was choking the barley.

No, she was right to stay.

The work needed doing and *bopplis* were born every day. There was nothing special about this birth. Nothing that needed her to be there more than she was needed in the fields. It promised to be a good crop. To provide them with an income to keep up with the rent and tide them over the winter. It would be careless to leave it unattended just to visit with her sister-in-law. Just to take her to the hospital. Anyway, the buggy would be crowded enough.

Quickly her hands reached for another weed as her eyes followed the buggy. It was fading into the distance now and the pace had not slowed. In fact, she couldn't be sure at this distance, but she thought the horse was cantering. A hand seemed to clench onto her gut and squeeze the air from her lungs.

Should she have gone?

Mary would be fine. So why did she worry? Her brother already had one child and Mary had shown no problems throughout this pregnancy. Yet *Daed* had been different this morning. Something about the look in his eyes made Rose wonder if she should have gone with them. Absently she reached for the weeds and plucked them from the field. *Gott* would take care of her family. He would see that all was right with the world. The way He sent the rain and the sunshine... but what about the weeds? He sent those too and without help, they would swamp the fields and smother the barley. If she did not tend the field, the harvest would be poor. Maybe it was the same with *kinner*. If you did not attend the birth, then things got out of hand. But her brother, David was there with her *daed*. They did not need her.

From across the field, the sound of a young girls' laughter floated on the breeze. Katie could always find something to laugh at. Right now she would be tending to Atlee, her brother's and Mary's two-year-old son. As another peel of laughter floated towards her, guilt flooded her stomach with bile. Katie was only eleven and yet she had taken it upon herself to look after Atlee. Rose ripped at the weeds, pulling them out as fast as she could and trying to blot out the thought of her sister doing all the work. No, that was wrong. Katie and her twin Lydia did the majority of the housework, the cooking, cleaning, and washing. They baked and roasted and kept the house as clean as it had been before their *mamm* deserted them. But they never milked the cow or chopped wood. They never plowed the fields or harvested the corn. Rose did those so her sisters didn't have to. She took on more of the farm as her *daed* got older. It had never been a burden. Reach and pull, reach and pull. The weeds grasped onto the dry soil and each time it seemed harder to pull them loose. It was as if they were fighting her. As if they defied her and wanted her to know she should not be here.

A cry rang across the field and Rose stopped. The sound of a child in pain filled her with despair. It took her back to the day their mother left. The sound of her sister's crying still haunted her dreams... almost as much as the look in her *daed's* eyes. Katie and Lydia were just six years old. Roseanna had been fifteen, almost an adult, and it had fallen on her to become the woman of the house.

A cut formed on her hand as it slipped across a ryegrass stalk. The weed seemed to wave before her, defiantly happy that it managed to draw blood. She bent down and wrapped her fingers around it pulling once more. For a second the tough grass held firm and tears formed in her eyes. How could she go on? Then the grass came loose and she almost fell backward.

This was her place. The crying from the field's headland had stopped. As always Katie had eased the child's tears. Now she would be bouncing little Atlee on her knee. Cooing and chuckling with him. Making him forget his *mamm* was not there. It had been just the same when their *mamm* left. Katie had taken over. She had looked after so much even though she was so young. She had held her sisters and soothed away their tears. While they clung to her, her little face filled with resolve as she dried her tears, Rose had felt so awkward. It should have been her doing those things but she didn't feel like an adult. All she wanted to do was drop to her knees and let Katie hold her. Then she had fled to the stables and watched the horses and the chickens. They had no worries, no stresses and they went about their day as if *Gott* provided everything for them. It had been a hard lesson. To know that she had to *let go and let Gott,* but she could not do it. On the outside, she carried on, but inside she was betrayed and hurt and she wanted to scream at *Gott* that it was not fair.

Gradually the years passed, but she never got over the hurt. It was like armor and she wore it to protect her from getting too close. If you let no one in, no one could betray you.

All the time Katie had been so small and yet so in control. Instead of crying, she helped others. At first, Rose thought of her as a child playing house but that changed. Soon she was so proficient. In a few years, she had taken over the cooking from Rose. Their meals had changed from burnt offerings to good, healthy, and tasty food. Rose had fled the house and found solace on the farm. The work was hard and yet easier... for her at least. It stopped her thinking, stopped her worrying, and kept her busy. There was no need to worry about anyone else when she worked the fields. No need to worry who she would hurt, or who would leave, or anything like that. The work just was, and she was out in *Gott's* glorious sunshine.

"You need to marry," *Daed* had said just last week.

Rose had nodded and told him she would see, but no *mann* had asked to drive her home from service in over a year. No *mann* wanted a woman who could work as hard as he could. They wanted a cook and a cleaner, they wanted someone to bear them children, and Rose could never see herself doing any of those things.

The crying was replaced by laughter, as she knew it would be. Katie was a wonder with children. It was something that always mystified Rose. How did you stop a *boppli* from crying? How could you look after something so fragile and how did you have the patience to put up with so much crying? In all her years she had shied away from *kinner*. Animals were easy to live with... but *kinner*? They were difficult, awkward, and so vulnerable she could not bring herself to even think about having one. Maybe it was because of the hurt.

As she moved along the rows, she thought about the hurt look on her *daed's* face. How he wanted to see her happy and no matter how she tried she couldn't explain that she already was. There was no need for a husband in her life.

For many hours she had prayed on this. It didn't matter nothing came to her. There was no answer to her hurt. Nothing would make her trust. What if she married a *mann* and then changed her mind? What if he changed his mind? What if they had children and she let them down? If she betrayed them as her *mamm* had? No, it was too much to bear, she was much better off as she was. Like this, she could hurt no one. Here, she did her work and talked to *Gott,* her life was just as He wanted. She was sure of it. The loneliness was something everyone felt, she was sure of it.

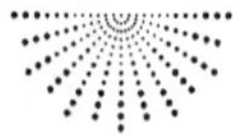

* * *

CHAPTER TWO

Therefore, since we have been justified through faith,
we have peace with God through our Lord Jesus Christ,
-Romans 5:1

* * *

SITTING on the grass at the side of the field, Katie Wagler bounced little Atlee on his toes. Somehow the child had picked up on the tension and she knew he was scared. It was a fear she had too. The look on her *daed's* face as he had helped Mary into the buggy had filled her with fear. David their brother was simply panicking, like all fathers to be. David's panic was natural but their *daed* had seen many births, and the set of his shoulders and the worried look in his eyes told her something was wrong, badly wrong. Apart from that, she sensed it, but she would keep these worries to herself. Carefully she bounced her two-year-old nephew and smiled at her twin sister, Lydia. They were so much alike in looks. With fine blonde hair, a face swamped with freckles, and big blue eyes that Katie hated. Often she felt they made her look vulnerable and childish. They suited Lydia but she wanted to be grown up. More than anything she wanted her own family, but at eleven she was much too young and so she did her best to look after the house and keep everything perfect.

Lydia was reading her Bible. It was something she often did when things got stressful. Her eyebrows were drawn down in concentration as she struggled with some passage. Lydia thought too much and all she ever wanted to be was a school teacher. A smile crossed Katie's face. Her sister would do it. She would be the best teacher if only she could muster a little more patience. Lydia often thought the world should mold to her point of view, her expectations, and she got frustrated when it didn't.

In the field Roseanna or Rose, as she insisted to be called, her eldest sister had escaped to her beloved crops.

This too was predictable, whenever there was any stress Rose would run to her fields. Rose worried Katie, she pretended to be so strong but there was something sad about her. Katie had tried to talk to her but she would never admit how hurt she was. Instead, she hid away from the world and pretended all was fine. She could be so pretty but she never smiled. It was as if all the joy had left her life and she was weighed down with guilt. Sometimes Katie heard her talking with *Daed*. He wanted her to court and to marry. At times, he even suggested an arranged marriage but Rose had flatly refused. Katie knew that their *daed* feared pushing Rose too far. He feared she would leave them, that she would leave the plain life and go live among the *Englisch*. It was his greatest fear and Katie did her best to reassure him. Sometimes she thought he saw their *mamm* in Rose and feared she too would abandon them. Katie didn't think that, she believed Rose was just afraid of commitment, but once she did commit she was loyal and fierce in her love. Never once had she let them down because she had taken on the role of their mother even when she hurt so badly herself.

A chuckle passed Katie's lips as she remembered how Rose had struggled. Visions of her stirring gravy as tears streamed down her face filled her mind. It had not been something that came easy to Rose and the gravy was usually thick and lumpy, but it still tasted good because it was prepared with love, and accepted with gratitude.

Katie rocked Atlee and wondered who she could talk to about finding Rose a suitor. Maybe she should make a pact with Lydia that they would get their sister married. That they would see a real smile on her face again.

Just as she was about to say something a cloud crossed over the sun and the day turned instantly darker. It was as if a storm was coming and she looked out at the field. Rose had stopped and was looking up. Katie knew she would be making a decision as to whether to stop for lunch. Already she had been working for three hours and her back and hands would ache from her labor. That was something else Katie worried about. The farm was not doing well and they could not afford extra help. Without farmhands, there was only Rose, their brother David, and their *daed* to work the fields. If this crop did not bring them in some money, they would be in trouble next year. A sigh escaped Katie and she wondered how they would cope.

"What is it?" Lydia asked.

Katie looked up to see the worry and fear in her sister's eyes. Putting a smile on her face to soothe her twin she reached out and touched her arm. "I just worry about the weather, is all? The last thing we need right now is rain." That seemed to work and Katie went back to her Bible.

Along the lane, Katie heard a horse and the sound of metal wheels on the gravel. Excitement went through her. Soon there would be another *boppli* to care for and she couldn't wait.

As the buggy turned into the drive, she knew it wasn't theirs. The horse was bigger, a light chestnut with a big white stripe down its face. It was the Bishop's horse. Katie stood to see what he wanted and just for a moment she felt a shiver go down her back.

ROSE SIGHED and stretched her back as a big black cloud floated in front of the sun. It instantly cooled the day and she looked up in trepidation. The last thing they needed was rain. It would stop the barley from ripening and make the harvest difficult. If it lasted too long it could even give the crop mildew. As she stared up at the sun, the cloud passed slowly over and the sun's rays came back just as strong. The sudden warmth engulfed Rose and forced a smile back across her lips. They were going to be fine. Soon the barley would drop its head and then it would turn golden brown and be ready to harvest. She had managed to secure a good price. It would be enough to keep them through the winter, to pay their rent, and maybe enough to hire a few farm hands for next year. If they could do that they could increase the yield and in a few years, they would be home and dry.

She knew her *daed* worried about the fact that he only had one son. The land was too much for David, especially as he never wanted to be a farmer. Her brother was a good *mann* but he was ill-suited to working the land. If their father passed... a shudder went through her as she imagined David letting go of the land. Who would take over the farm was her *daed's* biggest worry? For many years, all he thought about was who she would marry and would that *mann* make a good farmer? Rose had hated to disappoint, but she turned down any offer of marriage and flatly refused to court the men that her *daed* chose. There was nothing in the Ordnung to prevent her from working the farm, she knew because she had checked and that was all she wanted to do. What's more, she was good at it, as good as any *mann*.

Wiping a hand across her face, she went back to the task of weeding before she succumbed to pride. The work was good honest work, Godly work, and He would not have made her love it so much if He did not want her to do it. That had always been Rose's answer. Pulling up another weed she swallowed and wished she had brought some water with her. It was hot, thirsty work, but one more hour and she would go in for some lunch. Maybe they would be back from the clinic and then she would know if she had a new nephew or niece.

Across the fields, she heard the sound of a horse. Looking up, she saw a buggy coming in. With the gray roof and the black cab, it could be any buggy in the district but she recognized the light chestnut gelding that pulled the buggy. It was Bishop Amos Beiler's buggy. *What was he doing here?* A sharp pain thrust into her chest and the air caught in her lungs. Had something gone wrong?

Rose kept her eyes on the buggy as it turned into the yard and drove to the hitching rail. Amos got out, his black felt hat on his head. From this distance, she could not tell it was him, but the Bishop was tall and broad and it looked like him. For a second she resented this inter-ruption. The phone shanty was at the Bishop's house and *Daed* had probably called to give them the news. Did it matter? They would find out what the child was soon enough. Rose felt a flush of guilt hit her face at her uncharitable thoughts and she said a quick prayer of contrition. Then she saw Sarah the Bishops' wife climb down from the buggy and fear almost dropped her to her knees. Why would Sarah be here?

As she had the thought, she began to make her way across the fields. It was as if she was drawn there and the movement was automatic. Amos walked over to her sisters. Katie and Lydia were sitting on a blanket playing with little Atlee, her two-year-old nephew.

Katie pointed out across the field and the Bishop turned to walk towards her. Rose wanted to run, felt she should run but her legs would not obey her. They felt like rubber and slowed to almost a crawl. Across the corn Amos came, his black felt hat shading his face. Rose walked towards him whispering a prayer. "Even though I walk through the darkest valley. I will fear no evil, for you are with me; your rod and your staff, they comfort me. You prepare a table for me in the presence of my enemies. You anoint my head with oil; my cup overflows."

Amos was getting closer. His normal ruddy complexion was white. His hands were clasped together in front of him and there was moisture in his eyes. Rose felt her knees give way, she did not know what news he brought but she knew it was bad. In her heart and soul, she already felt the loss and a wail escaped her as Bishop Amos Beiler pulled her into an embrace.

"Be easy child," he soothed. "They are with the Lord now and all their troubles are over.

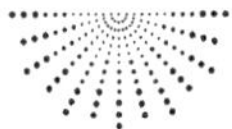

* * *

CHAPTER THREE

But even if you should suffer for what is right,
you are blessed.
"Do not fear what they fear; do not be frightened."
-1 Peter 3:14

* * *

Rose wailed as Amos pulled her into his shoulder. She did not know who was dead but she knew someone was and she knew it was bad. Never before had she seen Amos look so beaten, so lost, and all she could think about was why? Why had *Gott* done this to her? Who had he taken now? Was it the *boppli*? Was it Mary, her brother's wife? It didn't matter, once again she had lost someone close and she did not think she could cope.

Then she thought of Katie. Her little sister was so strong and a surge of guilt went through her. It seemed to be her only emotion today. Maybe she deserved this, maybe *Gott* was punishing her, but for now, she must be strong for Katie and for Lydia. Pulling away from Amos she wiped her eyes. "Who has been hurt?" she asked.

Amos looked at the ground and slowly raised his eyes to hers. They were old and tired, set amidst wrinkles that were tanned deep brown by constant hours in the sun. Once those eyes were a deep blue but today they looked faded like a dress left too long in the sun. One that was ready to be recycled into rags.

Amos was famous for his cheer. When he smiled it crinkled all of his face and gave him a jolly look that could brighten the darkest day. Only today he was not smiling. Today there was moisture in those wise old eyes and pain.

"Maybe we should go sit in my buggy?" he asked.

Rose looked across the field. She could see Sarah, the Bishop's wife sitting with her two sisters and Atlee. The young boy was climbing all over Sarah and for once

Katie didn't stop him. Even though Rose could not see her sister's face she knew it was as white as the Bishop's. Katie would know something was wrong. Perhaps she had already asked but more likely she was waiting to be told. It was her way to accept things as they came. Rose had never been like that. In that position, she would want to shake Sarah to find out the truth. She knew that she must have answers by the time she left this field, her sisters deserved that. Gulping down the lump that had formed in her throat she turned to Amos. "I need you to tell me what happened," she said without even a slight shake in her voice. If only the same could be said for her knees.

Amos took a deep breath and held her hand. "I am sorry child." Then he told her how her *daed's* buggy had been hit by a truck.

Rose felt her knees give way but somehow she stayed on her feet. "Who?" was all she could say and the word was barely a whisper.

"I am sorry child," Amos said. "From what news I have, your *daed* and *bruder* are with *Gott* now... your sister-in-law, Mary is grievously wounded."

Rose felt herself scream and cry and shout. In her mind, she beat her hands against Amos's chest and kicked and screamed out her pain. But she could not do that. She could not let her sisters see her pain. Right now she had to be strong for them so she let a groan of despair pass her lips and wondered what she could do. Indecision was like an anvil on her shoulders. It pinned her to the spot and held her in place. Part of her wanted to turn and run across the fields until she came to the city. There she could spend the next two years on her *rumspringa*. Maybe if she did that she could keep down the pain and hide from the hurt. Maybe if she did that she could one day forgive *Gott* for taking away so much of her family... maybe.

Across the field waiting patiently were her two sisters. They both needed answers but she did not know what she could tell them. Then a question came into her mind. "Will Mary survive?"

"I do not know." Amos said and Rose thought he had aged in even this few minutes.

A gasp of breath escaped her. "What about the *boppli*?"

Amos shook his head... "I do not know." A single tear fell from his right eye and rolled down his cheek before catching in the gray of his beard.

Watching that tear fall seemed to free her body and she started walking towards the edge of the field and her sisters. "Will you take me to the hospital?" she asked.

"I have ordered a car," Amos said as he hurried to catch up with her. "Sarah will stay with your sisters."

Rose stopped and turned to face him. "Do not tell them. Do not tell them until I come home, until we all come home tomorrow." She swallowed down the lump that threatened to choke her, she had to stay strong. "So far we do not know everything, maybe I shouldn't tell my sisters. Maybe I should just say there has been an accident?"

"I think that is a mistake," Amos said. "They already know something is wrong, but I am pleased to see how strong you are. Let the Lord guide your words and you will get through this."

Rose turned away. Right now she did not want to hear about the Lord. In her mind, he had abandoned her. Taking away both her parents and her brother... what more did he want from her?

As she rushed through the field, she could feel the corn as it brushed against her dress. Like thousands of tiny drum sticks tap, tap, tapping, growing faster and louder as she ran. She knew she was running across the rows and damaging the crop but she could not stop herself and soon she was getting faster and faster. The urge to grab a few things and flee was so strong that as she burst out of the field, she let out a small cry. In her mind, she dropped to her knees and screamed and shouted out her grief but instead, she calmly walked over to her sisters.

Katie and Lydia turned towards her and she knew she must stay. For now, she had to be strong for her sisters, but how would she cope? How would she look after them? As she had that thought, she remembered Katie and how strong she had been when their *mamm* left. Even though she was just a small child she had coped and taken on so many chores. At times it had been funny. This small child behaving as if she were their *mamm,* but it had given Rose so much comfort. If little Katie could cope so could she. The thing was, last time she had been playing at being a parent, this time that was what they would have to be. Rose looked at Atlee and she did not know how she would cope. What did she know about looking after a two-year-old? "Please Lord, keep Mary safe," she whispered.

Katie and Lydia were staring at her, the worry on their face was deeply ingrained. Rose knew she must be strong for them and she would be... at least for a little while.

Slowly she walked towards her sisters. Atlee was rolling on his back on the blanket, oblivious to the fact that his *daed* was gone. Tears started to form in Rose's eyes but she bit down hard on her lip and fought for control. As the taste of copper filled her mouth, she released her teeth, licked the speck of blood from her lip, and walked forward. Slowly she smiled at her sisters and nodded at Sarah. "Would you please take Atlee away for a moment?"

Sarah nodded and scooped the child up into her arms. Holding him against her chest he looked so angelic. Blond curly hair, blue eyes, and the chubbiest cheeks you had ever seen. Right now that angel's face was curled into a mischievous smile and he had not a care in the world.

Rose swallowed and sat down on the blanket opposite her sisters. They were so pretty. Long blonde hair was fastened up beneath their prayer coverings. Heart-shaped faces were covered with freckles and their cheeks glowed with worry. Rose felt her heart clench and her throat tighten. Swallowing hard, she tried to talk but the words would not come. Still, her sister's sat and waited, but she could see the way that Lydia's lips trembled and there was a slight shake to her hands. Katie had straightened her back. It was as if she were bracing for an assault and Rose hated what she was about to do.

"There has been an accident," Rose managed and she reached out and took their hands. Squeezing them gently she tried to give them strength for the awful words she had to say.

"What is it?" Katie asked.

Rose could see tears forming in both girls' eyes and she knew the longer she dragged this out, the worse it would be. Yet her mouth would not move, her lips would not form the words, and every time she tried there was a catch in her throat and it was as if she was suffocating and had to draw another breath.

"What is it?" Katie asked again.

"The buggy was..." She could not say hit with a truck. It filled her mind with the most awful picture and she could not do that to her sisters. "It was involved in an accident."

"Oh my," Lydia wailed and leaped into Katie's arms.

Rose watched as the twins hugged and out of the corner of her eye she saw the car pull into the drive. Amos walked over to it and talked to the driver. It was here to whisk her to the hospital but could she leave her sisters? Of course, she had to. Someone had to go and see what was happening, to make decisions. Maybe Amos could do it for her?

Katie and Lydia pulled apart and looked up at her. Suddenly they looked so young and so vulnerable and the weight of their fears seemed to crash down on her.

"*Daed* and our *bruder*... David are gone. They are with the Lord now."

"What about Mary and the *boppli*?" Katie asked. Now even her lips were trembling but she was trying so hard to be strong.

Rose wondered what she should say. Maybe she should lie and leave them with hope... but the look in Katie's eyes told her she could not. Katie would spot a lie and it would only make things worse. "Mary is very ill... I do not know about the *boppli*. I have to go to the hospital. I do not want to, I do not want to leave you, but Sarah will stay here. She will do whatever you need."

Katie and Lydia pulled her into their arms. Rose was not used to hugs, normally she was uncomfortable with them, but right now it felt good to hold her sisters. Gently she hugged them close and buried her face in their shoulders. Holding on to them she wanted so much to scream and wail, but she did not. Right now she had to leave and she had to stay strong until she had been to the hospital. Pulling back, she looked at the tear-stained faces. "We have each other and we have *Gott*," she said, even though she was angry at *Gott*, she knew her sisters needed Him right now. "We will get through this and remember our loved ones are happy now..." Her voice nearly broke and going on was the hardest thing she had ever done. Swallowing down her pain she continued. "We must not let them see us so sad."

Katie pulled away and nodded. Then she took her sister's hand. "We will be fine," she said but there was a catch to her voice and for the first time ever she sounded unsure. "Go and do what you must, but hurry back... we need you."

Those words cut through Rose like a knife. Just a few moments ago she was thinking of abandoning her family at such a difficult time. How could she? They would never do such a thing. They would stick by her and love and care for her no matter what. "I will," she said.

Slowly Rose got up and walked towards Sarah and Amos. "Do I tell?" She pointed at Atlee playing on the grass nearby.

"Leave that to me," Sarah said. "Go with Amos and *Gott* my child and may His strength be with you."

Rose felt the soft grass on her feet as she walked towards the house. She picked her shoes up from the porch and packed a few things into a bag then she got into the car after Amos. She waved as it pulled away from her sisters. They were hugging and crying and looked to all the world as if they were broken.

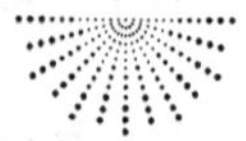

* * *

CHAPTER FOUR

*Therefore confess your sins to each other
and pray for each other so that you may be healed.
The prayer of a righteous person is powerful and effective.*
-James 5:1

* * *

SOON THE CAR pulled up outside the hospital. Rose had never been here before and her heart was pounding in her chest, her hands were slick with sweat and her stomach turned as if she had eaten some bad shellfish.

As she got out of the car, Amos turned and paid the driver. Slowly, his back bent more than usual, he led the way forward. There were people everywhere, it was even busier than the market, and she knew that a few of them were staring. Quickly she ran her hands down her apron. It was a little grubby from her work in the fields but not too bad. Why hadn't she changed it? Then she straightened her prayer covering and scuttled after Amos. The Bishop seemed confident as he walked into the tall and sterile-looking building.

It was so bright inside and people seemed to be milling about like ants. Amos pulled off his felt hat and held it in his hands. Rose followed but for a moment she wanted to turn and run back out of the automatic doors and into the warm sunlight. It was so cold in here, her skin was chilled by the air conditioning, and it made it hard to breathe.

Amos had gone up to a desk and was asking a woman in a blue and white uniform a question. For a second Rose stared at the woman. It was a dress with an apron over it and it looked so like her Amish clothes that she felt a little comforted. Maybe this was a good sign. Maybe everything had been a terrible mistake and her brother and *daed* would be sat in a bed somewhere. Soon they would be laughing and joking about the *Englisch* and their silly mistakes.

"This way," Amos said, guiding her arm.

Rose felt her heart pound at that simple touch as she was startled. Nodding to hide her nerves she followed him through the halls. There were people, trolleys, wheelchairs, and lines on the floor in different colors. There was a strange smell of disinfectant and decay. It was as if the place was soaked in chemicals and her nose could not separate them all out.

The place was so large and so confusing. Often they would stop at a crossroads and Amos would look up. Signs were everywhere and they seemed to contradict each other. Rose looked and tried to make sense of it all, but at times the writing all bled together. On and on they walked down so many different corridors but all of them looked the same. At last, they stopped and Amos took her to some chairs. A sign read 'ICU Waiting.'

"Wait here," Amos said. "I will find out what I can."

Rose sank into the chair and wanted to cry but she could not. Over a dozen people were waiting. Some of them had the same ghostly expression she could imagine on her own face. Some of them stared and whispered and some just looked bored.

Rose watched as Amos tried to attract the attention of another woman in a blue uniform that could be Amish but wasn't. She was sitting behind a desk, and at first Rose thought the woman was ignoring him, and then she realized she was wearing a headset and was talking to someone else. At last she smiled up at Amos. She was a pretty girl with a lot of makeup and long black hair swept back into a high ponytail. It seemed too frivolous a hairstyle for such a position and Rose wanted to do something but she knew she couldn't. At last Amos nodded and came over and sat with her.

"We have to wait," he said. "There is no news yet... she is still in surgery."

Rose felt a surge of joy. "That has to be a good sign... doesn't it!"

The look on Amos's face said it all. There was no hope, they were just waiting for the news.

Minutes passed into hours and people came and went. Some left with smiles on their face and joy in their heart. Others wailed as they were given the news, and some just seemed to collapse in on themselves as if all the air had been sucked out of them. That was how Rose felt, deflated. Breathing was too hard, too painful and she did not know how much longer she could go on. It felt as if a weight was crushing down on her chest and squeezing the air from her lungs. Desperately she tried to breathe but no matter how she tried, she could not draw a breath. A gasp escaped her and she could feel her throat closing even more. Rose knew it was panic and grief and knew she must calm down but it didn't help.

"Take deep breaths," Amos said and he put a hand on her back.

Rose tried, sucking in the air but it never seemed to reach her lungs, and then a doctor came into the waiting area.

"Roseanna Wagler," he called.

Rose looked around the room to see who was being called this time. A gentle hand touched her arm and Amos was helping her stand. Together they made their way over to the doctor. He was a tall, thin man with a tired-looking face and a touch of gray at his temples.

"Roseanna Wagler?"

"*Jah*, yes," Amos said. "I am Amos Beiler, a family friend."

"I'm Doctor Rhodes, I am so sorry about the tragedy that has befallen you today."

Rose looked up and tried to read the man's eyes. They were dark and blank. There was nothing in them to give her comfort.

"I can take you to see your sister-in-law now. Mrs. Wagler... is very ill... I cannot give you good news, but she will be awake shortly if you would like to talk to her."

"What of the baby?" Rose had said the words before she realized and once they were out she wanted to take them back. It would be too much to hear that the baby had died. After all this tragedy she could not take another blow.

A slight curl touched the doctor's lips. "The baby was born by cesarean section a short while ago. It is a girl... we believe she has an excellent chance of survival."

CHAPTER FIVE

* * *

*Jesus replied, "Truly I tell you, if you have faith and do
not doubt,
not only can you do what was done to the fig tree,
but also you can say to this mountain,
'Go, throw yourself into the sea,' and it will be done."
Matthew 21:21*

* * *

Rose followed Amos and the doctor through white,
double doors. They were strong and pushed back at her
as she walked through. For a moment she thought that
they would force her back but she gathered her strength

and pushed harder. Inside was a long corridor with doors leading off it. The doctor was already halfway down the corridor and Amos was looking back. There was sympathy in his old eyes, sympathy, and sorrow. Rose tried to straighten her shoulders and give him a smile.

It was a brave effort but never quite reached her eyes. In this foreign place, she felt lost and alone. *Daed* was supposed to deal with this sort of thing. He was supposed to keep her safe and make all the decisions. There was no way she could be left with a family to run. Then she brightened. Mary had come through the operation, her child had been born and there was every chance that Mary would recover. Rose ignored the look in the doctor's eyes and increased her pace. Mary was organized and an adult, she could look after everything and Rose would be fine.

The doctor had stopped outside a room. With a tired nod, he opened the door as Rose caught up. Amos went in first and Rose followed. The room was all white and seemed too bright for her eyes. There was a bed in the corner. Next to it was a machine with flashing lights and the pulse of a heartbeat that flashed across a monitor. Leads from the contraption lead down to the bed, but why? Rose thought the bed was empty and saw a door leading off the room. It would be a bathroom, Mary must be in there. A surge of joy lifted her spirit and she walked towards that room, but the incessant beeping of the machine pulled her eyes back to the bed.

At first she had thought it was empty, and then she saw Mary, and could not prevent the gasp that escaped her lips.

Mary seemed to have shrunk since this morning. Beneath the green blanket was a mere stick of a human with a battered face and a long gash down her right cheek. Rough black stitches held the angry wound together and pulled Rose's eyes like a beacon. Besides the stitches, her skin was deathly pale and had shrunk around her bones. That was the bits that were not cut or bruised. It seemed impossible to Rose that anyone could have suffered so much and yet had still survived.

"She may wake for short periods," the doctor said from across the other side of the bed.

Amos was standing looking down, and he looked away because Mary's *kapp* was missing. To Rose it didn't matter now, all that mattered was Mary was alive, and she would nurse her back to health.

Amos crossed the room and pulled his Bible from his coat, quietly he held the book to his heart, and he began to pray.

Rose wanted to join him, no she wanted to run, but her eyes were pulled back to the bed. A thin arm moved beneath the blanket, the other was bound to her side, and pain opened Mary's eyes. For a moment she stared past Rose and then her bloodshot eyes focused and Rose knew she had been seen.

"*Schweschder*," Mary whispered. "*Schweschder...*"

Mary's good arm reached down to her stomach. Rose could only imagine what she felt there but the panic on her face was apparent. Quickly Rose moved to the bedside and sat on a chair. It put her at a better angle for Mary to see. With a shaking hand, she reached out and took Mary's battered right hand in hers. There seemed to be no pain despite the fact that her hand was black and blue. "Your *boppli* is fine," Rose whispered. "You have a healthy *boppli* girl and she is going to be beautiful."

"A girl, I knew it would be a girl," the words were little more than a whisper and Rose had to lean in close to hear them.

Rose looked at the doctor, pleading with him, begging him, but he simply shook his head and then turned and left the room. As his stiff, white-coated shoulders disappeared through the door, tears prickled at the back of Rose's eyes but she fought them back. This was not the time for tears, this was a time for giving, and Mary needed her. If she could do little else, she could give support this day.

"David wanted a boy, but I knew," Mary whispered and there was a rattle when she spoke. "Where is my David, has he seen our *dochder*?"

Rose swallowed back her tears. "*Jah*, he saw her briefly but he had to lie down. He has been hurt."

Fear flashed across Mary's face. "Will he... and *Daed*, how is he?" A cough came out with the last word and it drained her.

Mary's eyes closed and for a moment Rose thought she had gone. A single tear fell from her eyes and was running down her cheek when Mary's eyes opened. There was more clarity in them this time. It was as if she rallied and fought the coming gloom.

"My David?" Mary asked. "Will my David be all right?"

Rose swallowed and said a small prayer. "He is fine, he wants to come and see you, but they won't let him at the moment. There is a problem with his leg and he will need an operation." It was a lie and the best she could come up with, but she hoped it would make things easier. "Maybe tomorrow he will come to see you and bring your *dochder*. I know he can't wait to show her to you, so rest now and soon you will be well enough to hold her in your arms."

Mary's eyes widened. "Will he walk again, will he be able to work?"

"He will be fine," Rose lied. "A few days rest and you will all be going home with your new *dochder*."

Mary relaxed and her eyes closed for a moment. Serenity crossed her bruised and bloody face and for a moment she looked like her old self. Gently Rose held her hand and tried to give what support she could.

For a few minutes there was nothing but the bleeping of the equipment and the slow labored sound of Mary breathing. Rose knew her time was coming and she whispered a prayer.

Mary's hand jerked in her fingers and her eyes opened again. "Tell me of my *boppli*?" she asked.

Rose was taken aback, it had not occurred to her to ask to see the child. She did not even know if she could see her, so what could she say? For a moment she opened her mouth but her throat tightened into a small stilted thing that would not let a word come through.

Mary stared at her, her eyes pleading and Rose thought of Atlee. In many ways, he hadn't changed much from when he was born. He had come into the world with blond curls and shocking blue eyes, chubby red cheeks, and what looked like a constant smile. "She is a happy baby, always looks like she is smiling. On her head is a mass of blonde curls and she has the chubbiest little red cheeks you ever did see. Deep blue eyes can capture you from across the room and she has a good pair of lungs. Almost screamed the place down, no doubt missing her *mamm*. You will see her soon, Mary of that I promise."

"*Denke*," Mary said. "I know what you are doing and I thank you for it. I know that I will see my *Gott* soon so I have a favor to ask. Look after my sweet girl, we chose the name Ester. Care for her and my sweet Atlee. I know things are hard, find a husband to give my *kinner* a family."

Rose felt a lump in her throat and tears in her eyes, what could she say? Then she knew that all she could do was agree. She would do her best to honor Mary's wishes. She would keep Ester and Atlee safe, this she promised. "I will, soon I will take her home but until I do you must promise me to rest."

Mary smiled up at her and gripped her hand tighter. "I am happy to meet my Gott, save my family."

Before Rose could say anything, Mary's eyes closed and the machines began to beep.

"No," Rose cried as a wall of grief, fear, and hopelessness crashed over her. She wanted to hold onto Mary, but the room was suddenly full of people.

Amos pulled her into his arms and she let out a wail of pain.

CHAPTER SIX

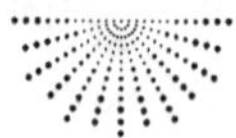

* * *

Now faith is confidence in what we hope for
and assurance about what we do not see.
Hebrews 11:1

* * *

6 MONTHS LATER.

Rose sat down at the table, the cup of coffee before her was almost cold, and outside the sun was just beginning to peek over the horizon. As always, her sleep had been disturbed. There were too many problems to deal with, too much to think about, and not enough time to do it all.

Sarah Beiler, the bishop's wife had been wonderfully helpful. Since the accident all those months ago, Rose had hardly had time to draw a breath. For the first month, the community had rallied around her. There was always someone in the house, always someone on the farm. The jobs were miraculously done and food was always appearing in the kitchen. The help with the children had been a Godsend. And little by little time had passed. For Rose, the grief hadn't.

Every day she wondered how she would cope and every morning she started the day with a prayer. Asking for help, asking for guidance, however, as the prayer continued her anger surfaced. Many times, she ended up berating *Gott* for the load he had given her. Why her family? Why take her *daed*? And why take her brother and Mary and leave this little *boppli* without a family? It was all too much and she couldn't get her head around it, though she had tried.

Katie and Lydia had been amazing. At first, all they could do was cry and Rose did her best to ease their pain. Holding them close, telling them everything would be all right was all she could do and she hoped it helped. Even though she felt a fraud and a liar doing it. How could anything be all right after what had happened?

As the sun began to rise, Rose knew she had to start work. The animals needed caring for and breakfast had to be cooked. They were weeks away from the harvest and the corn was full of weeds. If she didn't get them out soon, the crop would fail and they would lose the farm.

Dropping her head into her hands a single tear ran down her cheek. Angry, she brushed it away. What could she do?

Taking a sip of the cold coffee she went over her options. There weren't that many and none of them were good. One of the battles she had had to face was Mary's parents. In any normal situation, after such a tragedy, they would have moved in with them and everything would have been fine. Only it wouldn't have been!

Rose remembered Mary's last words, and how she begged her to look after the children. She understood it for Mary's parents were harsh and bitter and so strict in their doctrine that they stifled their daughter. Mary had only blossomed into the wonderful woman she was when she escaped her parents and there was no way that Rose would let little Atlee and the beautiful *boppli* Ester suffer that way.

Luckily, Bishop Amos Beiler and his wonderful *fraa* Sarah had agreed with her. They knew what Mary's parents, John and Susan Lapp were like. They accepted her decision to stay separate. Of course, they had pushed another solution on to Rose, gently, but it was something she couldn't do. *Not even for your family?*

The sound of a cockerel crowing brought Rose back to the present. She had to make a decision, she just didn't know how to make it.

Once more she went over her options. The one she would not take was to allow Atlee and Ester to go to his grandparents. The Lapps wouldn't take Katie and Lydia or herself. So it wouldn't even solve her problems.

The rent on the farm was overdue and she had no way of making the next payment until the crop was harvested. What could she do?

Of course, there was the solution that the whole district expected her to take. That was to marry. Good farmland was in short supply, land like the home that was all she had known was precious and highly valued. Amos had suggested a marriage but she couldn't bring herself to marry. If she were to allow a man into her heart, she knew he would break it. For a moment a vision of her *mamm* passed in front of her eyes, smiling and happy as she kneaded the bread dough in the kitchen. One day she had been there, the next she was gone. How could she do that?

Logically, Rose knew that it hadn't been that simple. There had been signs, but she still couldn't understand why her *mamm* had abandoned them.

No, marriage was not the way out of this. How else could she cope?

Then it came to her. One thing her *mamm* had been good at was quilting. In the loft, there were bags and boxes full of quilts. A decision was made, she would get them out and this weekend she would take them to the market. They would make enough to pay the rent for one month, maybe even two. That would tide them over. Now all she had to do was weed the crop and prepare it for harvest.

Put like that, it sounded so simple, but she knew that the quilts would take her one or two days and she didn't have the time to work on the crop. What could she do?

The sound of footsteps on the stairs made her wipe away her tears and put a smile on her face.

"Morning," Katie said as she rubbed the sleep from her eyes. Though she was still in her nightgown, she was wearing her kapp.

Rose swallowed the lump in her throat. Katie looked exhausted. She had taken on so much and never once had she moaned. Such courage made Rose feel weak. They would get through this together. That she promised.

"Morning," Rose said as she stood and walked to the stove. The coffee pot was still on and she poured them both a cup. "What would you like for breakfast?"

"I can make it, there's breakfast casserole leftover," Katie said with a smile. "Esther slept through the night. Let's hope that's going to continue."

Rose sat back down and took her sister's hands in hers. "Have I told you how proud I am of you?"

Tears formed in Katie's eyes and she shook her head. "We are family, we all pull together."

"No, you have done so much and you are so young. I would not be able to manage without you."

Katie smiled. "I have loved every minute of it and you do way more than you give yourself credit for. It would have been so easy for you to let Atlee and Ester go to their grandparents. I couldn't have coped if you had done that."

Rose was fighting back her own tears. She knew that Katie just saw her strong side. That she didn't see the sleepless nights and endless worry. She didn't see the times when Rose hid in the stables and cried. "We are family, and I would never abandon you."

"How far behind on the rent are we?" Katie asked.

Rose let out a gasp. Perhaps her sister was more aware of what was going on than she thought. "Two months... but I have an idea. I was going to get all the quilts out of the attic and take them to the market on Saturday. If you want to keep any... I understand. When I get them out I will let you go through them."

Katie clapped her hands together and jumped up. "That is a fantastic idea. You don't need to do it, Lydia and I can sort that out. Oh, I'm so excited, this is a new beginning." With that, she jumped up from the table and ran out of the room.

Rose, watched her go with a smile on her face. With such a wonderful family, she knew they wouldn't fail.

Somehow, they would keep the farm. Closing her eyes she whispered a prayer of thanks. Maybe *Gott* was on their side after all.

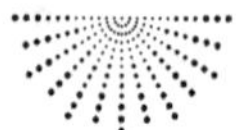

* * *

CHAPTER SEVEN

30 The fruit of the righteous is a tree of life,
and the one who is wise saves lives.
31 If the righteous receive their due on earth,
how much more the ungodly and the sinner!
Proverbs 11:3-31

* * *

ROSE PULLED another quilt out of the washer and into
the basket. Katie and Lydia had done a magnificent job
of getting all the quilts out of the loft. They had sorted
them into those that were in perfect condition and those
that needed washing.

Katie had not wanted to leave for school; however, that was nothing new. Immediately after the accident, the girls had been excused. Once it was time for them to go back, Katie didn't want to leave the children behind. She spent her days caring for Atlee and Ester and it broke her heart to leave them.

Lydia was happy to return. She was such a quiet girl and enjoyed time with her Bible and her romance novels. However, her true love was teaching and she loved to learn. To Lydia, the more she learned, the more she would know, and the better teacher she would become.

Rose was feeling much more optimistic this morning. These quilts wouldn't stop the flow of the river of debt that was drowning them, but they did offer a lifeline.

The heavy quilt was hard to maneuver, but she managed to get it into the spinner without getting herself too wet. There were three already on the line and only two more to wash. This had been a good morning's work.

Standing to stretch her back as she took in a big breath of air, she closed her eyes. The sound of the baby wailing jerked her back to the present.

Quickly she ran into the house to find Ester awake and unhappy. The scent in the air told Rose that a diaper change was in order. For a moment it was all too much once more, but then she felt a tug on her dress and looked down. Atlee was smiling up at her. The grin on his face was irresistible and she grinned back. Picking him up she spun him in the air and then placed him down.

"Well little man, are you going to help me change this diaper?"

Atlee's eyes widened and he shook his head. "I'd rather have a cookie."

Rose started to giggle and soon she was sitting on the floor holding Atlee and tickling him as they both giggled and laughed. Esther had stopped her crying and was looking over at them in astonishment. This only made Rose laugh more and more and soon tears of joy were running down her face.

A knock on the door was followed by Sarah Beiler walking in. "Oh my, are you all right?" Sarah asked as she crossed the room.

Rose got to her feet and without thinking, she handed Atlee a cookie. "I'm fine, this little man is just so funny." Rose pretended to come down to tickle him and Atlee ran off giggling.

Ester began to cry once more.

"You'll have to excuse me, Sarah, she needs a diaper change," Rose said.

"Let me do that, you make us some coffee, and here, I brought a coconut cake for you. Why don't we both have a slice, you look to be losing some weight." Sarah handed Rose a bag and crossed the room to the clean pile of diapers.

Part of Rose felt guilty. Should she really let the bishop's *fraa* do this? However, Sarah looked so comfortable and she knew she would be insulted if she refused, so she made them both some coffees and a slice of cake.

Soon they were sitting at the table and Rose bit into the moist and sweet coconut cake. "This is so delicious," she said.

"It is an old family recipe and both mine and Amos's favorite. Now, how are you doing?"

Rose was always planning in her mind how to answer that question. She would focus on the positive, on what was going well, and deflect any negative. Up to now, it always worked. Somehow, that all went out of the window. "We are failing." Rose's hand went to her mouth as if to pull back the words that had just betrayed her.

"That is all right. Once you recognize the problem it is easier to solve," Sarah said. "Now tell me all that you need help with."

Rose explained about the quilts and about being behind on the rent.

"The rent is no problem. You know that the district has a fund for this sort of thing. I will see that your rent is paid up to date," Sarah said.

Rose found herself shaking her head and she wanted to say no. Sarah, however, raised a finger.

"There is no shame in this," Sarah said. "Many have taken from the fund over the years and many, like yourself and your *daed,* have contributed over the years. This is what it is there for, accept the help."

"*Denke,*" Rose said as tears ran down her face. "Maybe I can use the money from the quilts to get some help on the farm?"

"That is something I wanted to discuss with you," Sarah said.

Rose felt the ice-cold touch of fear trace down her spine. Would they never stop forcing her into a marriage? Then she wondered, was it inevitable that she marry if she were to save the farm? Would it even be so bad? Her biggest fear was losing the land, letting her family down. After that, it was of having to spend all day in the house, maybe if she got the right husband then she could still work the land.

"I can see that you are still against the idea of marriage," Sarah said. "I totally understand, and I understand your reasons more than you know. You feel betrayed. But maybe, your *mamm* didn't betray you. Maybe she was called to something we can't understand."

"I just can't face the thought of marriage," Rose said. "But maybe I could get help, is there someone who could help me?" Then an idea came to her. "I could pay them with the profits from the harvest."

"That is a wonderful idea," Sarah said. "You have to decide what is more important to you. Would you marry if it kept your family together? Would you marry if it meant you kept the farm? Would you marry to help another? I do not think you're selfish, Rose, but I think you are looking at only the negative sides of a marriage.

There are many positive sides, even to a marriage that is not about love."

Rose took a bite of her cake to give herself time to think. Part of her wanted to shout and scream that this wasn't fair, but she knew that was childish. Part of her felt selfish for putting her own needs above that of her siblings. Would she marry to keep her family together? Yes, she knew if it came to that that she would. However, there had to be another way. "Do you have someone in mind?"

"I do, well Amos does. You know how he sees people that need help even when they don't know it themselves. Elmo Schrock lost his *fraa* two years ago. He has been working on an Englisch farm as he does not have land of his own. You both have something the other needs, why don't you meet him and see if you can help each other?"

Rose didn't know that much about Elmo. She remembered his *fraa* dying but she didn't know him well. The thought of allowing a stranger into her home was terrifying, but the thought of losing the farm, her sisters, and the children was even more so. A lump in her throat meant that she couldn't talk but she nodded her agreement to the meeting. Though she wouldn't tell Sarah this now, this would not be about a marriage, but about a mutual agreement to work the farm.

CHAPTER EIGHT

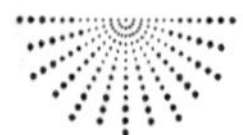

* * *

Do not be quick with your mouth, do not be hasty in
your heart to utter anything before God. God is in
heaven and you are on earth, so let your words be few.

Ecclesiastes 5:2

* * *

ELMO SCHROCK WALKED past the oak tree at the back
of his property. It had been a long day's work but he
hated coming home more than he hated the hard labor.
As he came around the side of the house he noticed a
buggy and horse stood there. A sigh escaped him. That
chestnut horse was easy to recognize, it was Bishop Beil-

er's horse. For a moment he thought about turning around and going for a long walk. If he did, perhaps Amos would leave him alone. However, he knew the man was persistent and maybe it would be better to get this over and done with.

Subconsciously, his hand went to his chin and tugged on what was no longer there. Each time he did that it brought back the pain, and he remembered his beautiful Susan and the child that would never be. The flare of anger went through him, why couldn't the bishop leave him alone?

Elmo walked around to the front of the property to find Amos sitting on the swing seat on his porch.

"It's a lovely evening," Bishop Amos Beiler said to him.

For some reason, that simple greeting knocked the wind out of his sails. The anger was gone and Elmo felt himself relax. Amos did not wish to hurt him, he was only trying to help. "That it is, Amos, what can I do for you?"

Amos stood and picked a bag up from the floor. "Sarah has a coconut cake for you, she's been baking a lot recently, keeping out of the heat. Perhaps I could share a slice and trouble you for a coffee?"

Elmo bit back a sigh and nodded. "Come on in Amos, I will soon have the kettle on."

It didn't take Elmo long to fire up the stove and boil some water. He almost wished it had taken longer for try as he might he couldn't formulate a way to tell the bishop to leave him alone. Well, not one that wouldn't get him in trouble. Though he was 25, tall and broad and much stronger than Amos, he still remembered being scolded as a child.

Running a hand through his thick black hair, he turned back to the stove. The kettle had boiled so he plucked it off and made them a coffee. Soon they were sitting at the table, a cup and a plate before each of them. Elmo knew that Amos would wait for him to eat, which would give him time to settle and relax before he began his talk. Though he wanted to ignore it, his stomach rumbled and he took a bite of the cake. It was moist and sweet and relaxed him.

"How are you doing?" Amos asked.

Elmo simply shrugged his shoulders.

"I know you are resisting my offer of marriage but there is a young woman who needs your help," Amos said.

Elmo raised his hands and shook his head. "I was married, I still love her, that is all there is to say."

Amos took a sip of his coffee and nodded. "I totally understand. But this marriage doesn't have to be about love, it can be about security and providing for others. It can be about working the land and sacrificing to gain what you love."

Elmo swallowed. Amos knew that the thing he wanted more than anything was a farm of his own. Would he marry to gain that?

"How is your job going?" Amos asked.

Elmo felt the lump in his throat, did the Bishop already know? "I have been given three months' notice. John Parsons son is coming home and taking over... but I will find another position soon."

"Hmm, that is interesting. What if a new position was available now, would you be able to leave straightaway?"

Elmo didn't know what to say. John had told him that he could leave straightaway if he got another position, but did he want to be forced into something he wasn't happy with?

"All I'm asking is you consider it," Amos said. "You would be helping out a young woman and four children. There is joy and satisfaction in such service."

"I could discuss it with them," Elmo said and knew that his cheeks pinked a little at the white lie. "I will meet with this person, with an aim to working on their farm, but this is not an offer of marriage, I want you to be clear on that."

"You have made that very clear. Just come and meet with Rose Wagler and take it from there."

Elmo felt his eyes widen. Why did it have to be Rose? She was looking after her twin sisters and a young boy and a *boppli*, how would you cope with all that noise, all that hassle? Perhaps he should tell the bishop that he didn't like children! "When would you like me to meet her?" he asked despite his doubts.

"How about tomorrow morning?"

"I will pick you up at nine," Elmo said, "but, as I said, I'm only interested in working the land. I do not want a family."

"I understand completely," Amos said but the smile on his face told Elmo that he didn't. The bishop was a wonderful man and could often see things that others couldn't, but his persistence in this matter was the last thing that Elmo needed.

ELMO ARRIVED at Bishop Amos's house early the next morning. For a moment he sat in the buggy waiting for the Bishop to come out, but then he decided that was rude. Climbing down he tethered the horse and walked up to the house.

"Good morning Elmo," Sarah called as she opened the door. "Can I get you a coffee or some breakfast?"

Elmo felt his stomach rumble at the smell of bacon and eggs that wafted through to him. "No, *denke*," he said.

Sarah laughed. "The rumbling of your stomachs tells another story. Take a seat, it won't take me many minutes."

Before he could say anymore Sarah had turned back to the stove and was cooking up the breakfast as he watched. Now he regretted coming early, or did he, the smell of the breakfast really was delicious and it would be nice to eat a meal with company.

Amos joined them and soon three plates of bacon and eggs were on the table along with copious amounts of coffee. "Tuck in," Sarah said after they had said grace.

As they ate they made conversation about the weather and the district and the service tomorrow. It was as if they were talking about anything but Rose Wagler and the farm. Elmo pushed his plate away. "*Denke*," he said. "You certainly are a good cook."

"*Denke*, I've had plenty of practice," Sarah said. "I know you are not really open to the idea of her marriage with Rose Wagler. Trust me, she feels exactly the same way. However, she needs help and you want to farm, look at what you can give each other not at the problems you foresee."

"I will do my best, but my heart is forever with my Susan." Elmo felt a tear forming in his eyes and he bit down on his lip to try and stop it.

Sarah put a hand on his shoulder and squeezed gently. "There was a time for everything," she said, "but your time for grieving is coming to an end."

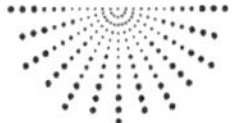

CHAPTER NINE

He guides the humble in what is right and teaches them
his way.
Psalm 25:9

ROSE HAD JUST SEEN her sisters off to school when she saw a buggy pull up to her house. Amos had brought her suitor. She was on her way to milk the cow, and her first thought was to hide in the barn hoping that he would not see her. Of course, that was childish, and whether he saw her now or later, this was something she had to face. Even though the money had helped with the rent, she still had to get the crop in and to do that, she needed help.

Plastering a smile on her face she walked out of the barn and could see Amos getting out of the buggy. On the other side, a man was getting out. Like Amos, he wore a felt hat and as he was behind the horse she couldn't see much about him other than he was tall and broad.

Amos saw her, and a smile crinkled up his face. "Good morning, Rose, how are you this morning?"

Rose swallowed down the lump in her throat and waved at him. If she shouted good morning, she knew her voice would not be strong enough to carry and she wanted the few seconds it would take to cross the yard to steady herself. As she walked towards them, the man came around the horse and into view.

"Good morning," Rose said as she studied the newcomer. He was an attractive man, fit from hard work in the fields and around 6 feet tall.

"Rose, this is Elmo Schrock, the man that Sarah spoke to you about," Amos said. "Perhaps we could have a coffee and a chat?"

Rose was still staring at the newcomer. He had a strong chiseled face with a dimple on his chin. She imagined he was a few years older than her but not as old as many of the prospects she had been offered. In many ways, she knew she could do worse but then he turned his eyes on her and felt a shiver. They were a steel grey and seemed to cut right through to her heart. There was something cold in those eyes, whatever it was she didn't want to find out.

"Rose, did you hear me?" Amos asked.

Rose turned to the bishop, there was concern in his faded blue eyes. She nodded. "Of course, Amos follow me." With that she led them into the kitchen sat them down and had soon prepared coffee and cake. It was the last of the coconut cake that Sarah had made and she felt a little embarrassed that she hadn't done any baking herself for as long as she could remember. A flush of guilt heated her cheeks as she thought about poor Katie. The child did so much and asked for so little. Would it hurt her so badly to marry if it would give her sisters a better life?

Rose sat down and poured them all a coffee, the silence at the table was so thick she felt as though she could cut it with a knife. This was just like Amos, he would wait them out, forcing them to relax and yet today it didn't seem to be working. Today she felt as if her panic was growing with every second. It was hard to draw breath, hard to sit still, hard to not scream at them to get out of the house and leave her alone.

"Well Rose, I can see how well you are managing," Amos said with a gentle smile. "The house is tidy and well cared for and I can see how much work you have put in on the farm, how are you doing?"

That took Rose off balance. She had expected him to tell her what was happening and not to inquire how she was managing. "We are managing well but there is much work to be done. I was hoping I could hire some help and pay with a percentage of the harvest."

"That is a very good idea," Amos said. "Of course, you could always consider marriage. Elmo here is looking for good land to work. Perhaps, the two of you could work together to build a home for all of your family?"

Rose felt as if someone was kneeling on her chest. It was so hard to breathe and the longer it went on the more painful it became. She had to tell him no, she had to let them know now that this wasn't acceptable or this awful man could take over her farm.

"Amos, I have an idea that might work better," Elmo said.

Rose was able to draw a breath and as she desperately drew in the air the two men's eyes turned to her. "I would like to hear your idea. I have no wish for a husband," she managed to gasp out the words.

Elmo nodded as if he agreed with her. "I too do not want a wife and I do not know how I would cope with a house full of noisy children. However, I am a hard worker and I am looking for land to make my own. I will help you with the harvest, and the planting in return for ½ share of the profits. I will keep what I need and the rest I will put aside so that in a few years I can buy this land from you."

Rose was on her feet before she realized, the empty chair clattering on the floor behind her. "Who do you think you are? This is my farm, my land and no one buys it off me." She didn't mention the fact that half the farm was rented and that if he really wanted to buy it he could approach her landlord who might easily let him have it. She didn't explain that if something didn't happen soon she would lose that land and would eventually have to sell the whole farm.

"Rose, I'm sure Elmo did not mean to insult you," Amos said as he stood and tried to take her hands.

Rose pulled her hands away. "I'm sorry, Amos, but this will not work. If I employ someone on my farm they have to know that it is my farm, my family's farm. The last thing I need is some man who wants to force me off my land. Now, if you would excuse me, I have work to do." With that, she turned from the table and left the room. Once she was outside Rose ran to the barn to hide. Tears were streaming down her face and her heart was pounding so hard in her chest that she thought it might burst free. Her stomach churned and she was suddenly dizzy.

Leaning against the stall she wiped the tears from her eyes and tried to control her breathing. The sound of Daisy, the milk cow moving in her stall brought her back to the present. Somehow, she would manage, she would find someone who would help and they would all get through this.

"I'm sorry, I made a mess of that," Elmo said as he drove his buggy back to the bishop's house.

"Do not think badly of Rose. She is hurting, has been hurting since their *mamm* abandoned them many years before. Since that time, she hasn't been able to trust anyone and she escapes to the land to make sense of the world."

"I do not think badly of her, in fact, after today, I admire her. When I came here, all I wanted to do was get this farm off her. After all, whoever heard of a woman running a farm?"

Amos chuckled. "It is not the traditional way, but I do not believe that *Gott* would frown on her behavior. In fact, I think He would be supporting her as much as He could."

"Perhaps He is, after all, He sent her you." As he drove the buggy back Elmo made a decision. He would help Rose and he would do it on her terms. Her spirit had impressed him and for the first time since his Susan died, he wanted to give to someone else.

CHAPTER TEN

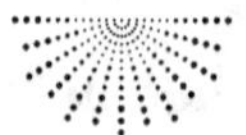

* * *

2 Consider it pure joy, my brothers and sisters, whenever you face trials of many kinds, 3 because you know that the testing of your faith produces perseverance. 4 Let perseverance finish its work so that you may be mature and complete, not lacking anything.

James 1:2-4

* * *

It was just after lunch on Monday that Sarah Beiler called around to see Rose.

"I am so sorry," Sarah said, "Amos is usually more intuitive than that. He's been having a little trouble sleeping and I feel he's not quite his normal self."

Rose felt a flush of guilt and she shook her head. "I'm sorry too, Sarah. I realize that Amos is only trying to help me. Unfortunately, Elmo is not the sort of man I need. I need someone I can work with. Someone who will take my direction and understand that I know a lot about this farm. I know that some don't like me working on the land but it is the life I have been given. I have prayed a lot on this and I believe this is where I am meant to be."

"I believe you are right," Sarah said.

Rose felt a huge sense of relief to hear that, part of her had believed that the bishop and Sarah did not like how she lived. To hear Sarah say she agreed was like a weight lifting off her back. If only more in the district would be as forgiving.

Sarah offered up a chocolate cake and they enjoyed a slice with a coffee. After that, she helped with the washing and played with the children before leaving.

Little Ester was exhausted and ready for her nap. Rose was hoping to get an hour in the fields while she slept. Atlee could play along the field edge and she would be able to keep an eye on him while Ester would be in her bassinet in the shade.

It took only a few minutes to get prepared, with the bassinet in one hand and Atlee holding her other she opened the door and let out a shriek.

Standing in front of it, his hand raised was Elmo. He seemed to tower over her and just for a moment the raised hand looked like a threat. Rose stepped back shielding the children behind her. What was it with this man? Was he trying to be the end of her?

"I am so sorry," Elmo said as he stepped away from the door and lowered his hand. "I was just about to knock."

"I am not selling my farm to you!" Rose said as she placed the bassinet down and clung onto Atlee.

"No, forgive me, I came to apologize for my bad behavior yesterday. I do not want a *fraa* but that does not mean I do not think you are a wonderful person. You would make someone an amazing *fraa*. It's just that I still love my Susan and it would seem like a betrayal to marry someone else."

Rose swallowed down a lump that threatened to choke her. That was not what she had expected and she suddenly felt that she would like to know this man. Her own *mamm* had left her and their family and yet this man would not leave the memory of his *fraa*. She understood now why he had said what he said, for many times she said the wrong thing when all she was trying to do was protect herself. "*Denke*, for the apology, it is very appreciated."

Rose felt very strange and wondered if she should offer him a drink. Would it be appropriate? Would there be any point?

"I wanted to do more than apologize," Elmo said. "I am willing to work on your farm under your terms if you still need the help?"

Rose was filled with hope and she had a sudden urge to shout out her joy. Instead, she nodded. "I would like that very much. When can you start?"

"Well, I am off today. Tomorrow morning I would have to go and speak to my boss. There is a possibility I could come back after that or he may make me work some notice. Is that of any use to you?"

"It is great. I was just about to go out and do some weeding. Ester should be asleep for at least an hour and Atlee will be happy playing at the side of the field. If you join me we could get a lot more done. But what about the financial side of things." Her eyes lowered to the floor and once more she was finding it hard to speak. It was difficult to tell someone of her shame, especially when she expected him to work for her.

"It's okay," he said. "Amos told me that you are not flush with cash. I can work until the harvest and take ¼ of the crop. If that is acceptable?"

"That is acceptable," she said and held out her hand to shake on it as she had seen her *daed* do many times.

As he took her hand his handshake was firm and strong but not overly so. He did not crush her fingers just to prove a point.

"I have another possibility as well if you are interested?" he said.

Rose had just been about to pick up the bassinet and show him out to the field. She stopped and nodded.

"Susan's family would be happy to babysit for us while we work in the fields. I understand you might not want this, but if it helps, they could take the *kinner* for a couple of hours."

Rose felt a huge smile cross her face and then she felt guilty. How could she be so happy at the thought of getting rid of the *kinner*, even if just for an hour?

"You don't need to feel guilty about that," he said. "Many parents have someone look after their children if they need to work for a few hours."

Rose let out a sigh of relief. He was right. "Would they really not mind?"

"Not at all, they would love it."

"Well, not for today because Katie and Lydia will be home from school soon and they would worry if the children were not here. However, I would love to take you up on that a couple of times a week for just a morning. I could get so much more done and then I would be able to spend more time with them later."

"Then let us get to work, show me what you need me to do," Elmo said.

They spent the next two hours pulling out the weeds from the field closest to the house. Rose was a little embarrassed at how bad it had got. She had kept on top of a lot of the farm but this field had been the field she had been in the day of the terrible accident. Something had kept her from it. Some superstition that if she came back to work in it that something awful would happen. Only, it didn't. In fact, the opposite happened. Elmo was strong and competent and between the two of them, the work went so quickly.

"Any chance of a drink?" Elmo asked after they had been working for two hours.

"Of course, I will make some lemonade. Katie and Lydia will be home soon, would you like me to bring it out here or you can come up to the house?"

Elmo stood upright stretching his back and reached out to the sky. Taking off his hat he rubbed a hand through his thick black hair and glanced around the field. "There is not much more to do, if you don't mind I will keep working while you make it?"

"Not at all, I will be back shortly."

Rose left the bassinet where it was for Ester was still sleeping and she didn't want to wake her. She would be able to see from the kitchen and Elmo was there anyway. Little Atlee had found a stick and was cantering around on it as if it was a horse. "Would you like some lemonade, Atlee," she asked.

He turned on his pretend steed and pranced about as if he was a fine and spirited riding horse just out for a run. Then he gave a whinny and chased after her, overtaking her and racing her back to the house. Rose felt herself chuckle. It was so good to see him laughing and enjoying himself. Maybe life would hold some joy for her too, one day.

Once the lemonade was made she grabbed some glasses, a tray and the jug and set off back to the field. As she glanced over it she couldn't see Elmo and a moment's disappointment stabbed into her chest. Had he deserted her already?

Then her eyes went to the bassinet as she suddenly feared for Ester. There, under the shade was Elmo. He was looking down at the *boppli*. Rose hurried out the door and across the field, her protective nature always fearing the worst.

Elmo didn't hear her coming and as she approached Ester began to cry. With a look of wonder on his face, he leaned over and pulled her from the bassinet rocking her gently until the crying stopped. It was a wonderful sight and not quite what she expected. Wasn't this the man that said he couldn't cope with nosy children?

Rose put the lemonade tray down and Elmo turned toward her.

"She was fussing, I just thought I'd pick her up," he said.

"You are good with her," Rose said.

"What are you doing?" Katie shrieked as she came running across to them.

Rose suddenly realized she hadn't mentioned Amos and Sarah's wish to see her married, and her sisters knew nothing about Elmo. How would Katie take this?

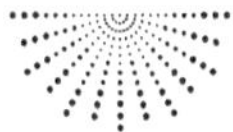

* * *

CHAPTER ELEVEN

19 See, I am doing a new thing! Now it springs up; do you not perceive it? I am making a way in the desert and streams in the wasteland.

Isaiah 43:19

* * *

KATIE RAN up to them and pulled Ester out of Elmo's arms. "Who is he and what is he doing?"

"Katie I'm so sorry," Rose said. "This is Elmo and he is helping me out on the farm. Ester was crying, he was just helping."

Katie was hugging Ester to her and it was clear from the look on her face that she didn't know whether to be still angry or whether to be embarrassed. That was when Rose realized how much she had put on her young sister. Katie had become a mother to the children and Rose had let it happen because it helped her so much. But was it healthy or fair? She guessed that the next few moments would answer that question.

Katie stepped from foot to foot, fidgeting like she always did when she was nervous. Her eyes flicked to Rose and then to Elmo and then back to Rose and her mouth was opening and closing but no words were coming out.

"It is okay," Rose said. "Ester is fine and so is Atlee. Where is Lydia?"

"She got a new book from her friend today, she rushed inside to read it," Katie said, her cheeks were flushed and she was finding it hard to meet Rose's eyes. Rose smiled at her and nodded. Katie seemed to relax and she looked up at Elmo. "I'm so sorry, I didn't mean to shout at you, I was just worried about Ester."

"That's okay," Elmo said. "I can see how much you love her and that is all that matters. I promise I will never hurt her, but I can't promise I will ignore her if I hear her cry."

"That's okay," Katie said. "I'll take her back to the house and start dinner."

Normally, Rose would've agreed. Normally she would've had to have agreed for she would have been working in the field for another few hours. But tonight she realized that she was putting too much pressure on the girls. It was her turn to cook. She glanced up at Elmo and he nodded.

"You go take care of your family," Elmo said. "I'll have a glass of lemonade, I'll do another half an hour and then I'll see you tomorrow if I can, if not I'll call around tomorrow night and let you know when I can start."

Rose felt tears prickle at the back of her eyes. How had she been so lucky? And to think that she had wanted to send Elmo way. "*Denke, denke* so much."

"It is my pleasure."

ELMO WORKED in the fields for almost another hour. All the time he was working he couldn't stop thinking about Rose. How much had she been through? It was amazing that she had done as much work as she had. He could see the guilt and the hurt that she was suffering. She believed she had let her siblings down. That she had let them take on too much and that it was hurting them. Elmo didn't see it that way.

At times the hurt of losing his Susan and their unborn child was still too much to bear. After it happened he had been a wreck. At six months after the tragedy, he had still been unable to cope, and yet here was Rose, she had lost so much and yet she had managed so well. The house was clean and tidy, the children's clothes were clean. Though Rose looked a little slim, the rest of the family looked well-fed and happy. As he worked he had looked around the farm and he was amazed at how much she had managed to do.

She hadn't kept up with everything, the barn door needed mending, some of the fences could do with repairing and there were other jobs here and there, the sort of jobs you only did when you had time. The harvest would have been impossible for her alone. There was only a short season to get the corn in before it was spoiled and there was no way one person could do it. Between the two of them, it would be difficult but he knew of a couple of friends he could ask. And suddenly, it was important to him that this harvest was a success.

That Rose could keep her farm. It was a strange feeling to have when he was so desperate for land himself, to wish that she could keep this land seemed contradictory... but he did.

CHAPTER TWELVE

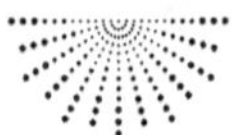

* * *

5 And hope does not put us to shame,
because God's love has been poured out into our hearts
through the Holy Spirit, who has been given to us.
Romans 5:5

* * *

IT WAS the following morning when Rose was out hanging washing on the line that she saw Sarah Beiler walking by. For one moment, she wanted to run and hide but she knew that would not work. If Sarah wanted to talk, then she would talk no matter how long it took. For the time being, she had decided she wouldn't mention anything about Elmo. Their agreement was still new, and she had no idea if he would stick to it. In many ways, it was asking a lot of him.

"*Gut* morning," Rose shouted.

"*Gut* morning, Rose, how are you?" Sarah stopped and came over to the fence.

"I'm doing okay," Rose said continuing to peg washing on the line.

Almost instantly, Sarah was at her side and together they made light work of hanging out the sheets.

"I know he came across as very cross and uncaring, but Elmo is a nice man. Maybe you could simply court him for a while and see where things go?" Sarah asked.

Rose couldn't help but feel annoyed. Why did everyone want to see her married? She had to bite down on her lip to prevent herself from speaking her mind. What she wanted to say would not be suitable for the bishop's *fraa!*

Sarah laughed. "I know, the interfering old busybody should leave me alone."

Rose blushed. "I never would have said that."

"I totally understand, just know that everything that and Amos and I do is out of love. We have prayed extensively on this, and we believe that you could be happy if you let a man into your life. Do not think of it as losing your independence, but as a way to keep it. Anyway, I will not push you any further towards Elmo... but I can't say I won't stop looking for the perfect man for you." Sarah patted her on the back before turning to continue her walk.

For the rest of the morning, Rose worked between the house and the field. When Ester was fussing, she worked in the house and when the *boppli* slept she took advantage and escaped to the fields.

She was hoeing the vegetable plot while Atlee was riding around on his pretend horse. Suddenly an idea came to her, she had seen the horse's head on stick toys at the local store. Once the quilts were sold, she would get him one. The thought of the smile on his face kept her going for most of the morning.

Rose looked up as the sky darkened, a huge black cloud was drifting across. The last thing she needed was rain. She closed her eyes and said a prayer to keep it moving.

"*Gut* day, Rose," Elmo said.

Rose's hand flew to her chest as her eyes burst open. Taking a breath she tried to calm her heart.

Elmo was laughing and she was surprised at how much it softened his face and those eyes that she had once thought were cold.

"I'm so sorry, I seem to keep scaring you. I promise it is not intentional."

Rose chuckled and shook her head. "It's not your fault, I was just praying that the weather would hold until we got the harvest in." Rose noticed the two elderly people who stood behind him and raised her eyebrows.

"These are my parents, Lucy and Mervyn, if you would like they will take the *kinner* for the afternoon?"

Rose looked at the smiling couple and for a moment her heart froze. Could she really let the *kinner* go with them, strangers? Of course, she knew these people, she had seen them at service and lived among them all her life, but could she trust them with her *kinner*? Then she realized that was the first time that she had thought of them as such. It was quite a shock and it must have shown on her face.

"We are quite happy to look after them here for the day," Lucy said. "If that is easier for you?"

Rose looked her over. She had a soft face and smiling grey eyes just like her son. Mervyn's hair was going grey as was his long beard, but there was a smile on his face that just made her want to relax. "Would you mind, really?"

"Not at all," Lucy said. "We can keep you supplied with drinks all day too. It looks like it's going to be a hot one."

Soon the children were introduced and Rose and Elmo set off back to work.

"When were you thinking of starting the harvest?" Elmo asked.

"The furthest field will be ready this week. Unfortunately, one of my team threw a shoe and has gone lame. I'm hoping he'll be better in time but if not I'm a little stuck."

"I'm pretty good with horses, do you want me to have a look?" Elmo asked.

Rose felt tremendous relief. As much as she loved working on the farm, the big Belgian draft horses made her a little nervous. It was silly, they were gentle beasts and very calm but hauling up their hooves was something she was never comfortable with. Especially, when one of them was hurting. "I would like that," she said.

"Lead the way."

Rose checked on the children as they made their way to the paddock behind the barn. There were six big chestnut draft horses and the lighter and smaller buggy horse that was a bay.

"It's Rupert over there in the corner," she said pointing to the horse which was favoring its near hind leg.

Elmo opened the gate and approached the horse. It was easy to see that he was confident and competent and the horses all came to him. "Well, Rupert, let's have a look at you." Elmo ran his hands across the horse's flank down its quarters and down further to its fetlock, just above the hoof. Standing up he turned back to Rose. "He has a bit of swelling there but it's nothing too bad. I have some medication at home. I'll nip back in a bit and get him some. If he's not better in a day or two then I can borrow a horse to get the harvest started."

"You are so good with them," Rose said.

Elmo gave her a big smile. "I spent a lot of years working with them. In my last job, working for an *Englischer*, it was all tractors. They are fast and efficient but it doesn't feel the same working the land with something mechanical as it does with a living being. Now, where would you like me to start?"

Soon they were working in the back field. Rose loved how they work together. It was as if he could anticipate her next move and he was there to help her. As the day progressed, she felt her stress, her anger at the loss of her family, and a little of her hurt start to ease.

At 3 o'clock they stopped for a lemonade. Lucy had come down with a tray for them along with a piece of pound cake. She must've made it herself for there had been none in the kitchen. They talked together for a few minutes and then she returned back to the house.

"I'm just going to have a few more minutes," Rose said.

"I'm pleased about that," Elmo said with a chuckle. "You set a hard pace, I'm struggling to keep up."

Rose laughed. "I doubt that very much."

"I get the feeling you were praying about more than just the weather... this morning," Elmo said.

Rose sighed and straightened her kapp. It was a habit of hers when she was nervous. "Sarah Beiler is still pushing me to find a husband. I know she only means well, but I have too much on my plate to be thinking about courting. However, I can't see her leaving me alone until I am."

Elmo laughed. It was amazing how much it softened his face and the dimples on his cheeks and chin made him look young and carefree. "I get much the same from them." He chuckled once more and shook his head as if he was thinking about something. "Would you be up to a little bit of subterfuge?"

Rose shrugged her shoulders. "What do you mean?"

"We could pretend to court, it would get them off both of our backs and give us time to get this harvest in."

"Would that be honest?" Rose asked.

"What is courting if not getting to know the other person? We will be getting to know one another, if after a few months we decide we are not suitable, then that would be quite normal."

Rose nodded, of course, he was right. "I'm willing to give it a try."

"That is great," he said with a big smile on his face. "We will work in the fields as we are and on Sunday, I will pick you up to drive you all to service." With that, he put down his glass and walked back to the field.

Rose followed him. There was a feeling of excitement inside of her, a feeling of something good coming. She had never been driven to service before and it felt good to be asked. Shaking her head, she had to remind herself that this was just to keep Sarah and Amos off their backs. Still, she wondered what it would be like to go with him to service.

CHAPTER THIRTEEN

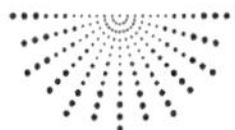

* * *

Take my yoke upon you and learn from me,
for I am gentle and humble in heart,
and you will find rest for your souls.
Matthew 11:29

* * *

ALL WEEK ELMO returned and worked hard. He stayed long hours and took much of the burden off Rose. Some days his parents came for the children, others Rose managed them as she always had. By the third day, she was looking forward to him coming. It was much less lonely working in the fields when you had a like-minded person with you. They would talk as they worked and even more so when they stopped for a break. He had been bringing his own lunch but Rose had told him that the least she could do for him was make some for him.

"I'll go make our lunch," she said as the sun shone high overhead.

Elmo looked up and smiled. "Shout at me when it's ready."

Leaving him, she picked up the bassinet and walked up to the house. Ester was ready for a feeding and needed her diaper changing. It wouldn't take long, she was surprised at how good she had gotten at it. In fact, caring for Ester was now second nature. She almost did it subconsciously.

Once Ester had her bottle, she set about making some ham and cheese sandwiches. They would make a hearty meal with a few pickles and she had a little bit of the poundcake left that Lucy had made. Once it was ready she walked to the back door and rang the bell. In the field, Elmo looked up, and just for a moment, she wondered what it would be like if he was here all the time, if they really were married.

The thought surprised her and heat flushed her cheeks. Rushing back inside she dampened her face with some water. The last thing she wanted was for him to think she was infatuated with him.

Outside, Elmo rinsed off in the tub for the horses. As he came in, she handed him a towel and pointed to the table.

"I think we can start the harvest tomorrow," he said. "I checked Rupert this morning and he is ready to work."

"That is great news, but eat your lunch. You have worked hard and need to rest."

In silence, they ate the sandwiches, drank strong coffee, and munched on the pound cake. It wasn't an awkward silence, but more one made out of hard work and the need to recharge batteries.

"Would you like anymore?" Rose asked.

"Did I see some raspberry muffins?" he asked and then looked a little ashamed and shrugged his shoulders. "Sorry, I should never have asked."

"Of course you should, you are working so hard. I did make some raspberry muffins last night... however, I have to admit, I'm not as good a cook as your *mamm*.

You're welcome to try them and I hope you won't be disappointed."

"*Denke,* I'm sure I won't be."

Rose got up to serve him one of the muffins and as she did Ester began to squeal. Rose dropped the plate on the counter and rushed across the room only to see Elmo picking the *boppli* up. There was a look on his face that she had never seen before as little Ester stared into his eyes and changed her cry to a smile. The look was one of awe, one of wonder and it softened his face even more.

Rose went back and got the muffin and brought it back to the table. "Would you like me to take her?"

Elmo sat down still holding little Ester and she was sure that there were tears in his eyes. He shook his head and swallowed. "Do you mind if I keep her for a while?"

"Not at all, she stopped crying with you a lot quicker than she would with me." Rose chuckled and felt warmth by the sight in front of her.

"You never had *kinner,* did you?" Rose asked.

This time she was sure there were tears in his eyes as he shook his head. "I lost my Susan in the birthing bed. We would've had a daughter, but it was not meant to be."

"I am so sorry," Rose said and she reached across and placed a hand on his. "I can't imagine how awful that must've been."

"I was angry at *Gott* for so long. Angry at everyone, even at myself. I couldn't see the point in going on."

"And yet here you are, you did go on and you have done so much to help me," Rose said. The words touched her for she had felt that same rage, that anger and disappointment that everything had been taken from her. All the time she should have looked at what she still had, instead she only worried about what she had lost. For Elmo, it must have been even harder, for he was alone.

"When I first came here, all I could think about was getting your land," he said and he looked her straight in the eyes.

Was he wanting her to be angry with him, it didn't matter she couldn't be.

"It was your strength that helped ease my anger. I knew what had happened to you, as does everyone in the district. I can't imagine the strength it must've taken for you to go on. For you to take on this family and the farm and to keep it all as well as you have done. That night, I felt so ashamed and I decided I had to help you. I want you to know that I am doing this for you and that I will never try and take your land from you."

"I'm ashamed to say I was not strong," Rose said. "When my *mamm* left I fell apart and I escaped to the land. My *daed* was getting older and less able to cope. It meant I had more work to do, it also meant I could be there with him. However, I didn't hold the family together, that was Katie. She's so strong that she puts me to shame."

Elmo was shaking his head. "Don't think like that. If you had spent all your time in the house, you would never have kept up the rent and you would have lost half of your land. With only half left, you would not be able to support the family. You are strong beyond belief and you have inspired me."

"Thank you," was all that she could manage.

"I have never spoken to anyone about my family before," he said. "About losing the *boppli*. Of course, some know, but they are few. It felt good to talk about it. I have always shied away from *kinner*. It was too painful to see them and know what I had lost. Now in one week, I have picked this little muffin up twice and I can't believe how good it feels."

Rose chuckled. "When Mary asked me to take care of Ester, my first thought was to run. I was terrified. What did I know about looking after a *boppli?* But, somehow I managed. I don't think I would've done it without Katie and Lydia. Lydia is quiet but she still works hard and she causes me no trouble whatsoever."

"It is hard. The pain of grief is like drowning," Elmo said. "At first it is intense and desperate, you are struggling for breath. You're been sucked under by the sheer awfulness of it. In time, you are lulled into a sense of numbness, but then a big wave will come in, and once more you are gasping for breath and fighting the pain. However, I can tell you that it gets easier. I now remember the good memories as much as the bad, and yet the pain can still hit at unexpected moments."

"I know exactly how you feel and I do understand. We have to remember that this was *Gott's* will and that they are in a better place," she said for she would not admit that she still felt such anger. It was hard to pray, she still did it but if she were honest she had lost her faith.

He adjusted Ester in his arms and she chuckled and tried to hang onto his finger. "For a long while, I was so angry at *Gott.* Why would he do such an awful thing to me? I lost my faith, it is only now that I feel I can return to that faith."

"I have felt similar, not all the time, but at times. How did you get over it?"

"Who said I'm over it?" he said and then chuckled. "All I can do is remember the good times, and that you had the joy of that person in your life. Yes, it hurts, but it would've been worse to have lived without them."

Rose had to agree with him there. She had spent many years with her *daed* and brother and Mary. There were many good memories she could remember, maybe she should start and do that?

CHAPTER FOURTEEN

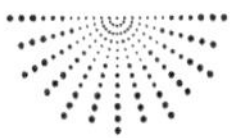

* * *

"I have told you these things,
so that in me you may have peace.
In this world you will have trouble.
But take heart! I have overcome the world."
John 16:33

THEY STARTED the harvest and managed to get one field cut and bailed and even though it was hard work, Rose had never been so happy. After her conversation with Elmo, she had taken some time to remember the good times. She had spoken to Katie and Lydia and they each brought up their favorite memory of each person. It had been a night full of laughter and tears but it felt like a new beginning.

Elmo had decided he was going to come in on Saturday morning and do some mending on the barn. Rose had told him he didn't need to, for she was going to the market to sell the quilts. However, he said he had nothing better to do and he was really enjoying the work.

The buggy was not big enough for them all so they had to take a cart. They piled the back with the quilts and Rose and Atlee sat upfront while the twins sat in the back with little Ester fastened firmly in her crib.

Elmo had made sure that they were safe before they left.

The market was crowded and buzzing with *Englischer* and the quilts were highly sought-after. Even though she had priced them high, they sold like hotcakes. Soon they had made so much money and all the quilts were gone. Rose decided they deserved and needed a treat. There had been no money for anything since the accident and yet things were looking up.

"Who would like an ice cream before we go back?" Rose asked.

A chorus of yes and me along with big smiles made her feel like it was all worth it.

When they got back, she would get Atlee his new horse.

It was Sunday morning and Rose stared out of the kitchen window watching Atlee ride his wooden horse around the garden. It was amazing how much joy the toy had given him and Rose was starting to feel some hope after so long feeling nothing but despair.

Behind her, Lydia was reading her Bible, and Katie, as normal, was looking after Ester. It had only been a week since Elmo had joined them, but already Rose was able to spend more time looking after the home. At first, she thought she would resent it. However, she was surprised to find that she enjoyed the time. It was good to see the twins able to be children again. Even if Katie was determined to still be the mother of the family.

This morning Katie had prepared a list of what she needed for meals for the week. Rose had told her that she would take over the cooking. The look on Katie's face had almost made her laugh. Her sister didn't want to give up her role. Perhaps she was enjoying it, however, Rose was not going to let her do too much.

"Stop fiddling with your kapp," Lydia said and Katie and Lydia giggled.

Rose steadied her hands and turned mock angry eyes on her sisters. It only made them giggle more and she couldn't help but smile at the sound. When was the last time the house had been filled with laughter? She couldn't remember.

"You know he will come and get us," Katie said. There were more giggles.

"He will come and drive *you* to service," Lydia said.

"Elmo is just helping us out, and, he's driving us *all* to service," Rose said, and yet there was a feeling in her stomach of excitement. She had to stop this, this man was not looking for a wife. If she let her emotions get carried away with her, then she would be hurt once more. Somehow, she didn't think she could cope with that.

The sound of voices outside pulled her back to the window. While she had been concentrating on her sisters, Elmo had arrived in his buggy. Outside, he was talking to Atlee. The two of them were laughing and she couldn't help but join in when Elmo pretended he was also riding a horse and cantered around the yard.

"Elmo is here, are you girls ready?" Rose asked.

With much giggling, they said they were and they all left the house to find Elmo waiting for them.

He was still playing with Atlee and Rose was surprised at how handsome he looked with a smile on his face. *Stop it!*

"Good morning ladies," Elmo said and helped them all into the buggy. The two younger girls were helped into the back seat. Then Atlee went on the middle of the front seat and Elmo took Rose's hand to help her up.

That brief contact sent a flush of warmth up her arm and into her stomach. *What was wrong with her?*

CHAPTER FIFTEEN

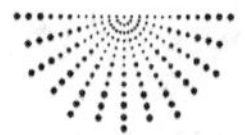

* * *

May the God of hope fill you with all joy and peace as you
trust in him,
so that you may overflow with hope by the power of the
Holy Spirit.
Romans 15:13

* * *

ALL THROUGH THE SERVICE, Rose knew that Lydia and
Katie kept looking at Elmo. At times they were giggling
and she had to elbow them to make them be quiet. The
last thing she wanted was for Elmo to feel uncomfortable. She did not know what she would do if he were to

leave them now. Ice-cold fear ran through her veins. It could happen, just when she was getting herself back on her feet, it all depended on a man she hardly knew.

Bishop Amos Beiler always gave services that seemed to reach into your heart. Today was no different. He spoke of trust and acceptance of *Gott's* will. As he talked of letting others into your heart, Rose looked across and saw that Elmo was looking at her.

Heat flushed her cheeks and she lowered her head quickly. It was not quick enough to prevent a giggle from Lydia and Katie.

Once the service was over Rose took *boppli* Ester from Katie and let the children go play with their friends. Ester needed a feeding and would soon need her diaper changed. Rose made her way to the side of the barn where it was quiet and she could have some peace.

Once Ester was fed and changed, she rejoined the crowd to find that most people were already eating. Lydia, Katie, and Atlee were sitting at the table near Elmo and some of their friends. She noticed that the seat next to Elmo was empty and that there was a plate of food. Who was he expecting?

At that moment, Sarah Beiler saw her and came over. "I guess you changed your mind about Elmo?" Sarah said with a knowing smile on her face.

Rose knew that her cheeks were flushing. "He has been such a big help, we thought we may as well see where things go."

"I am so pleased for you. He is a really good man. Now, go on he saved you a place." With that, Sarah patted her on the back and went to speak to someone else.

Had he really saved her place? Well, she guessed there was only one way to find out and she went over.

As she arrived at the table Elmo stood and pulled out the chair. "I wondered where you'd gotten to," he said.

"I just had to change and feed Ester. I didn't want her causing too much fuss."

"Lydia helped me get what she thought you'd like. If you need anything else I'll fetch it for you. Come, sit down and eat. I will take Ester for a while." With that, he took the *boppli* from her arms.

Rose sat down and saw that the plate was piled with all her favorites. There was fried chicken and coleslaw and small new potatoes. There was also a slice of coffee cake for all of them. A lump formed in her throat as she imagined what it would be like having this treatment all the time. Quickly she shook her head. She must not think that way, this was just a ruse to get people to leave them alone.

And yet Elmo looked so at home with Ester. Cooing and giggling to the *boppli*, he soon had a big smile on her face. There was no doubt he was a natural.

Once the meal was over, people gradually began to drift away and it was their time to leave. Once more, Elmo held out his hand to assist her into the buggy. Only this time, their eyes met. They no longer looked cold, but warm and welcoming. *What was wrong with her?*

Once they were back at the house, Katie took *boppli* Ester inside and Lydia and Atlee followed. It left them alone for a few minutes.

Rose wanted to say something for the silence was no longer comfortable but awkward, and Elmo was shifting on his feet. It was obvious he wanted to go, but also as if he wanted to say something. She had to break the tension. "*Denke* for taking us today. I spoke to Sarah and she accepted what I said."

"It's the first time I've traveled to service with anyone since it happened," he said and a dark cloud of sorrow passed over his eyes. "It felt good to talk to people. Of course, I've always had my family and my friends... but that is not the same."

Rose wasn't quite sure what he had said. Was he saying that he wanted to court her, or was he just being polite? Part of her wanted to ask, but she decided not to. After all, she didn't want to push him. "How have you found your first week?"

"I've loved every minute of it and I can't wait to come back."

"I hate to say it, but I've enjoyed working with you, too."

He lowered his eyes and cleared his throat as if embarrassed. It looked like she had said too much, that she had read things wrong. "I should be going, I will see you early Monday morning." With that, he climbed up into the buggy and was gone.

Rose was left feeling cold, confused, and worried. *Where was this going?*

When she went inside the house, she was surprised to see that Lydia and Katie were staring out of the window.

They turned around and giggling went to sit at the table. Rose decided she would do some baking. It was nice to have some free time, even on a Sunday. Before Elmo, even though she hated working on the Sabbath, she had no choice.

"I'm going to do some baking, what would you like?"

Lydia and Katie giggled once more. It was so good to see they were like children, but she pretended to be annoyed. "What's so funny?"

"What would Elmo like you to bake?" Lydia asked laughing so hard she was almost crying.

"I believe he likes your raspberry muffins," Katie said.

"Raspberry muffins it is then," Rose said deciding that if she couldn't beat them, she may as well join them. But as she made up the mixture she felt a little sad. It was obvious from his reaction that Elmo wanted to keep this as a business transaction. How quickly she had changed from the woman who never wanted to be married to one who suddenly saw herself with this amazing man. Of course, as she had been told so many times, no man would want to marry the woman who works the farm.

CHAPTER SIXTEEN

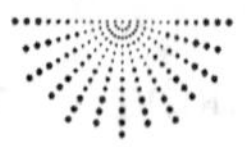

* * *

For God did not give us a spirit of timidity,
but a spirit of power, of love and of self-discipline.
2 Tim 1:7

* * *

THE WEEKS SEEMED to rush by and Elmo became more and more a part of the scenery. Rose knew that her siblings were beginning to treat him as family and it worried her. Though they spoke, often for hours, and often about very personal things, he had not made any attempt to make the courtship real. Rose was certain that once he was established, he would leave them and go his own way. Luckily, she would now have enough money to employ some farmhands. They would manage, she would keep her farm and the family would be secure. Only, she didn't know what it would do to her heart.

This week was the final week of the harvest. After that, there would be less work to do and Elmo would've had his payment. There were jobs around the farm that needed doing, and the fields would need to be prepared for planting in the spring, but Rose was feeling down knowing she wouldn't see as much of him. Would he still be there when springtime came?

She was making their normal ham and cheese sandwiches. It seemed to be his favorite and she did them at least twice a week. They were going to eat in the shade of a tree, a big old river birch. It was one of her favorites and she grabbed a blanket and the basket with the lunch and a pitcher of lemonade.

Calling for Elmo she took the picnic down to the tree. He soon came and joined her. As always, they chatted about things in the district. About how the *kinner* were getting on and what jobs needed doing on the farm. Once the sandwiches were eaten they always took a short time to just relax and talk. It was Rose's favorite part of the day.

"How is Ester? Has she done anything new this week?" he asked.

Rose laughed. "You are such a natural with her, you would make such a good *daed*." After she had said the words she felt guilty and bowed her head to hide her shame.

Elmo reached over and put a finger under her chin raising her head so they were eye to eye. "You do not have to tiptoe around me anymore. I feel healed and I am ready to move on."

Rose held her breath. What did he mean? A seed of hope was planted in her heart, was he moving on with her?

His fingers caressed across her cheek and his face was coming closer and closer. Still holding her breath Rose closed her eyes. She had never kissed a man, was he about to kiss her? Her heart pounded and hope built inside of her, but then his touch was gone. Opening her eyes she saw him stand.

"I'm sorry, I have to go." With that, he turned and almost ran back to the stables.

Rose couldn't move, what had just happened, and why had he run? Though she wanted to go after him, to talk to him she found she couldn't move, so she sat there and watched as he harnessed his horse and drove away.

That evening she tried to smile as she prepared the meal, and when she was asked what was wrong she told them she had a headache and was going to bed.

Elmo did not come back the next day and Rose was devastated. She had behaved like a child. Closing her eyes and opening her mouth expecting this man to kiss her. Yet no doubt he had just been wiping something off her cheek. She knew that he must be horrified. After all, nobody was interested in the woman who worked in the fields.

The harvest was almost complete and Rose knew that she could manage the rest of it on her own, she just didn't want to.

As she was preparing the horses, Sarah Beiler came to see her. "Have you heard about Elmo?" she asked

"I pushed him too far," Rose said. "He left, he doesn't want to come back I'm sure of it."

"I'm sure that's not the truth," Sarah said. "His *mamm* has been ill and they have been trying to hide it. Amos worked it out and realized they needed money for medical attention and didn't want to ask. If something happened between you, that is not why he hasn't come back, his *mamm* was taken to the hospital last night. He sent a message for me to come and tell you and said that he would be back once she is better."

"Oh my, I am so sorry." Rose felt tears running down her eyes and suddenly Sarah was pulling her into her arms.

"Let's put these horses back in the paddock and come and have a talk with me," Sarah said.

"I have to get the harvest finished," Rose said.

"Amos will see to that, he will soon find a few people to help you, but now you need to talk and tell me what happened."

Before she could say anymore, Sarah had taken the large horses from her and lead them back to the paddock. Rose could only stare as she expertly dealt with the large beasts. Removing the harness and turning them loose. "Now, coffee and cake are needed," Sarah said as she guided Rose up to the house.

As they drank and ate Sarah managed to get Rose to open up. She confessed how the courtship had just been a ruse and how over time she had fallen deeply in love with Elmo. It was only as she said the words that she realized it was true. Then she explained what happened. How they were talking, and she thought he was going to kiss her, and how he fled in terror.

Sarah took her hand in hers and shook her head. "He did not run in terror. I think maybe it brought back memories. Men are funny, he was no doubt feeling guilty and was unsure and he panicked."

"Are you sure?"

"I think so and you will find out soon. He came to see us to use the phone shanty to call for a car to take them to the hospital. He asked me to come to see you and to tell you that he was sorry and that as soon as his *mamm* is better that he will be back. He said that he would explain everything when he comes back and that you must not worry."

"Why didn't he tell me his *mamm* was ill?"

"I think it was because he had seen that you were recovering. He knows how much you have come to care for his parents and he was trying to save you the hurt," Sarah said.

Rose knew she had to save him the hurt too. "I want to see him. Would it be wrong to go and visit? Would you even know how?"

"Amos will go with you. I will stay here and take care of the *kinner*," Sarah said.

"Quickly I must prepare the buggy and go to Amos."

"There is no rush," Sarah said and then she smiled and got up. "I will help you."

As they walked out of the house a buggy was trotting up the lane and Sarah waved and called. The horse pulled up to a halt and Sarah asked them if they would take Rose to see Amos. Of course, they agreed.

Rose had tears running down her face as the buggy trotted along the road. Soon she was with Amos, he sat her down and provided her with coffee while he arranged the car.

What would she say to Elmo, would he want her there? She knew it was time to gather her courage and tell him how she felt. Either he felt the same way, or he didn't.

This not knowing was too much, but was it fair to say this when his *mamm* was ill?

Amos came back in from the phone shanty. "The car is arranged it will be here shortly. I can see you are troubled. I know you care deeply for Elmo. Do not worry, he feels the same."

"At this time I shouldn't be worried about my feelings, but about his *mamm*."

"I am sure Lucy will be fine, and I'm sure he will be glad of your support at this time."

Rose hoped that Amos was right, she didn't think she would cope with any more tragedy.

CHAPTER SEVENTEEN

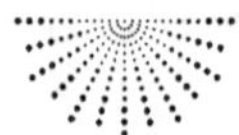

* * *

Consider it pure joy, my brothers and sisters,
whenever you face trials of many kinds,
James 1:2

* * *

IT SEEMED like forever before the car arrived and Amos helped her in. She had only been in a car once before and under normal circumstances, she would've either enjoyed the journey or been terrified. Today, she simply closed her eyes throughout it and prayed. She prayed for Lucy and that she would recover, and she prayed that Elmo would appreciate her support.

"We're here," Amos said.

It was over a two-hour journey to the hospital by buggy and so she was surprised when they arrived in next to no time.

"Am I doing the right thing?" Rose asked.

"I know you are my child," Amos said as he guided her into the hospital.

Rose had never been on her rumspringa and she was surprised at the size and busyness of the hospital. It was almost overwhelming and she was so pleased that Amos was with her.

Amos guided her through the crowded hospital as if he had always been there. He stopped to ask at reception where to go and then competently led her through the maze of corridors until they arrived at the waiting area. Elmo was there and Rose froze. Suddenly, she knew she had done the wrong thing. She should've waited at home for him to come back and she just wanted to turn and run. *What was wrong with her?* Every time there was a problem she got this urge to run.

Before she could do anything Elmo turned and saw her. His eyes opened wide and for a moment she thought he would be angry but then he smiled. Getting up he ran across to her and swept her up into his arms and hugged her close. It felt wonderful to be in his arms, it felt safe and where she should be.

Elmo quickly pulled back and turned to Amos. "I'm so sorry Amos, I know my behavior was inappropriate but I got carried away."

"I think I can forgive you this once. Now, how is your *mamm*?"

"The operation has been a success. She's not out of the woods yet but the doctors are hopeful. If she wakes up she will be fine," Elmo said.

"I am so pleased to hear that," Rose said. "Your *mamm* has become... well, she has just been so good to me and I care for her deeply."

"Why don't I go and talk to Mervyn while you two grab us all some coffees," Amos said and with that, he walked away.

Elmo guided Rose back down the corridor, and around a corner there was a machine that he could get coffees from. It looked very strange to her but he seemed to know what he was doing and he inserted coins and waited for the machine to make this strange noise. Then a cup dropped down and filled with various liquids. She wondered why there wasn't just a kettle, but there again what did she know?

Elmo got 2 cups and took her to one side. There were some chairs and tables and he sat down.

"Should we take this back for your *daed* and the Bishop?" Rose asked.

"I think Amos was giving us a chance to talk. Sit, I have so much I need to say to you," he said.

Rose felt her throat go dry and she didn't know whether to speak first. She could see he was swallowing and that he was nervous about speaking and so she jumped in. "I'm so sorry I thought you were going to kiss me. I am naïve, I have never kissed a boy and I know I made a mistake. I really enjoyed working with you and I don't want to spoil things between us. I can carry on working as if nothing happened if that is what you want." The words had just streamed out of her and she could see that he was amused.

"It's not what I want," he said.

Rose gulped. It looked like she had upset him worse than she thought. Desperately she sought for the words that would make him understand.

"It's okay, Rose," he said. "You were right, I was going to kiss you and I was wrong to do so. It is wrong for me to be kissing you when we are not married. It is wrong in so many ways. That is what stopped me. I really wanted to kiss you, but then I remembered Susan and I felt so ashamed that I just ran."

For a moment he stopped and took a sip of his coffee.

"I understand," she said, even though she didn't. How did he feel about her?

"I can't tell you how much I have enjoyed working with you," he said. "How much I have loved spending time with Ester, Atlee, and the twins. In my dreams, I imagined we were a family and then I remembered that you were famous for not wanting a husband. I am sorry I pushed you and promise I won't do it again. Will you let me come back and work with you, please?"

All Rose could do was nod.

"That is good, maybe we should take the coffees back to the bishop and my *daed*."

Elmo got up but Rose knew she had to tell him how she felt. She reached across and took his hand. "Please sit for a moment more. I'm trying to gain my courage, to tell you how I feel, and if you don't feel the same way please do not be embarrassed."

Slowly he sat down and she was still holding his hand. "I never thought I would feel this way again," he said.

"I love you, Elmo," she said.

Elmo reached across the table and took her face in his hands and put a delicate and tender kiss on her lips. "I love you too Rose, would you make me the happiest man alive and become my *fraa*?"

"Yes, yes I would love nothing more," she said.

CHAPTER EIGHTEEN

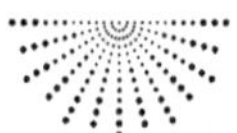

* * *

Blessed is the man who perseveres under trial,
because when he has stood the test,
he will receive the crown of life that God
has promised to those who love him.
James 1:12

* * *

WHEN THEY TOOK the coffees back to Amos and Mervyn they found them not in the waiting area but in the hospital room. Lucy was awake and though she looked weak and tired she was happy. Mervyn quickly explained that she was out of danger and would be coming home in a week.

"Come here you two," Lucy said. "Let me look at you, you make such a lovely couple. Would you make an old woman happy and give me some good news."

Rose and Elmo shared a glance and they nodded.

"I would like to announce that Rose and I are to be married," Elmo said.

On the bed, Lucy clapped her hands. "That is such good news. Now, I can really call those wonderful *kinner* my family. You have both made me so happy. Now, I need to plan a wedding."

"Just be careful you don't go and tire yourself out too much," Mervyn said and a ripple of laughter went around the room. They all knew there would be no stopping Lucy when she was in planning mode.

* * *

THAT NIGHT, when Amos took Rose home she found Sarah Beiler playing games with the children. It was such a wonderful sight and she realized how far they had come.

"How is Lucy?" Sarah asked.

Rose quickly gave her the news that Lucy was fine and would be coming home soon. Once more, she was fiddling with her kapp and finding it hard to sit still. Katie began to laugh, and then Lydia joined in. Atlee laughed just because everyone else was and *boppli* Ester started to chuckle too.

"Are you going to let me in on the joke?" Sarah asked; however, there was a glint in her eye and Rose believed she already knew. "Amos, do you know?"

"I'm just here to take you home, my love. I'm not getting involved," Amos said with a big smile on his face. "It is joyous news, though. Come on Rose tell them."

"Well erm, Elmo and I have been talking," Rose said. What was she going to say? What if her siblings were happy as they were and didn't want her to marry? How could she turn their life upside down once again?

"Do you love Elmo?" Atlee asked and everyone laughed.

Rose was laughing too, so much that tears were streaming down her eyes. Through the chuckles, she managed to tell them, "Yes, I do, is that a problem?"

"We've known for ages," Katie said.

"We've been guessing between us on how long it would take you to realize," Lydia said.

"I only just realized," Atlee said, "did you know Sarah?"

Sarah nodded and once more a burst of laughter went around the table. It was cleansing, healing laughter. It was blowing away the last of their sorrow and welcoming in a new joy.

"He has asked if he can marry me," Rose said before she could ask if that would be a problem everyone was on their feet jumping and shouting and cheering and she guessed she no longer needed to ask.

"Where will we live?" Lydia asked, "and does he have any books?"

Another burst of laughter went around the room. "We haven't spoken about it but I'm hoping we'll live here," Rose said.

There were lots more questions and Rose answered as many as she could.

"Okay you monkeys," Sarah said, "time for bed." With that, she hustled the *kinner* upstairs and left Amos and Rose alone.

"I'm sorry to be keeping you," Rose said.

"Do not be, Sarah will be so happy to have had your news, and to spend some time with the *kinner* is just sheer joy for her. I am pleased too, you and Elmo make such a perfect couple, I know you will be very happy."

Sarah came back downstairs. "They are all tucked up in bed. Now, the wedding. As you have no family, the wedding will be at our house and I will arrange every-thing for you."

Rose opened her mouth to protest but both Sarah and Amos shook their heads. So instead of protesting she pulled them both into her arms and hugged them tightly. "*Denke, denke* so much," she said.

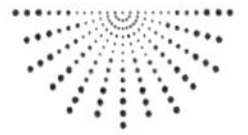

* * *

Dear friends, let us love one another,
for love comes from God.
Everyone who loves has been born of God and
knows God.
John 4:7

* * *

IT WAS three months later and the wedding day had arrived. Rose was preparing herself in Sarah's bedroom with her sisters by her side. They would be her *newehockers* and look after her during the wedding. Sarah and Lucy were also there. They had promised to look after *boppli* Ester and had done everything for the wedding. It was just such a joyous day and Rose could not wait.

In the intervening months, Elmo had put his house up for sale. The sale hadn't quite gone through yet, but it soon would, and the money they raised was enough to buy the land that they currently rented. They had spent many evenings talking about the farm and what they planned to do. At one time, Rose would've thought this would have annoyed her. However, it felt good to bounce ideas off another person and to get their input. It felt good not having to deal with every problem herself. She hadn't realized quite how lonely she had become.

The *kinner* were happy too. Katie was still determined to be the *mamm* but she had managed to slow her down a little bit. It had helped when a local boy took an interest in her and started calling around. She was still a little young to be courting properly, but Rose knew how sensible Katie was and she had no worries.

Atlee was as happy as always and he made Elmo promise that he would always play horsey with him. Elmo had been happy to make that promise and most nights they spent at least half an hour chasing each other around like a pair of mad things. It made Rose smile to see them so happy.

"Get your head out of the clouds," Katie said, "they will be waiting for you."

Katie and Sarah had made her dress. It was a sky blue, a beautiful color, and even though it was almost the same as her everyday work dress, it felt special. For a moment her nerves failed her. How many would turn up? After all, she had always been thought of as strange. She was the woman who worked the fields and no man wanted anything to do with her. Would they turn up to support her wedding, or would they stay away?

"No getting cold feet," Lydia said. "He loves you, and we love him, so get down there and get married."

"I guess I'd better," Rose said.

Before she went, both Lucy and Sarah pulled her in for a hug. "We are both so proud of you," Sarah said. "You have worked so hard to keep this family together and you deserve your happiness. Go and start your new life."

Rose made her way down the stairs, through the kitchen, and across the yard with the girls and ladies following her. Mervyn was waiting at the door and guided her into the barn. "You have made me so happy," he said as she went past him.

When Rose entered the barn she was amazed to see that it was full. Everyone had turned up and they all looked happy to see her. Maybe it was time to let go of her lack of confidence and truly return to her faith.

Standing at the front, Elmo looked so handsome in his black suit with the bow tie. How she loved him and how she was so pleased that she had let go of her anger and bitterness.

Rose walked up to Elmo and took his hand. Amos acknowledged them and began his sermon by speaking about the sanctity of marriage. Even though the wedding service took a long time, to Rose it felt like minutes and Amos was announcing that they were man and *fraa*.

Once the service was over the celebrations began and Rose and Elmo made their way through the people, receiving congratulations as they went. Rose was so pleased that everyone was so nice to her and she realized how much she had kept herself apart since her *mamm* had left them. All this time, she had been so angry and hurt that she had forced people away. How lucky she was that this wonderful man had come into her life and shown her that not everyone would let her down.

Soon they were escorted to the corner table, or eck, as it was known. It was a table of honor and the feast began. Sarah and Lucy had done them proud, but Rose felt as if she could hardly eat.

"I never thought this would happen to me," she whispered to Elmo.

"I never thought I would love again," he said. "In many ways, I am pleased that your life happened the way it did. You are a beautiful woman and if you had not been hurt, you would have been married years ago and I would never have the joy of you being my *fraa*."

"You say the most wonderful things, husband. I love you so much."

"And I love you. We have our whole lives ahead of us and the farm to work, so you must eat to keep up your strength. I will not let you be slacking, now that we're married."

Rose wanted to kiss him so much, part of her had feared that he would expect her to be a traditional *fraa*, it looked like she had no need to worry. Elmo understood her and loved her for who she was. What more could anyone ask for?

Rose closed her eyes and whispered a prayer of thanks, for the wonderful life she had.

Anna Sutter had a good life, all things considered. *Gott* had graced her with a loving *mamm* and *daed,* and a younger *schweschder* who seemed to shine as brightly as the sun.

When there were so many people in the world who had not even one person to care for them, she knew that she was blessed beyond measure. That was what made her pervasive sadness all the more difficult to bear.

She lived in an Amish community called Faith's Creek, along with the rest of her *familye.* It was the place she had been born, as had her parents before her. She had *nee* doubt at all that it would be where she lived still when it was finally time for her to go to be with *Gott.*

She thought it was probably one of the loveliest places in all of the world, although she had nothing to compare it to, and she was happy enough to stay there for the whole of her life. It wasn't where she was that made her unhappy, it was who she was inside, and she thought that must be a good deal worse.

She was a slight young woman, slender trending on the side of frail. Her deep chestnut hair was always up under the covering of her *kapp*. She was careful never to let a single strand stray out of place if she could help it. She did not like the idea of giving people a reason for her to be seen.

Her eyes were wide and almost as dark as her hair, and her skin was as pale as a fresh container of cream. Against the dark hues of the blue dresses that were her daily uniform, she worried that the extremity of her fairness made her stand out like a white sheet fluttering across a night-darkened sky. The thought alone made her tremble with dread, and it made her more than a little weary to venture outdoors more than was strictly necessary.

Perhaps worst of the long list of things she believed weren't quite right about her, was the fact that at twenty-years-old, she remained unwed. Not only was she still unmarried, when many of her peers had already begun their own happy *familye's*, but she also had nary a prospect or hope of being courted anytime soon. It seemed to her that, aside from her always loving parents and *schweschder*, nobody in Faith's Creek wanted her or would really care if she were suddenly gone.

"Such a foolish way to think," she chastised herself as she tugged mercilessly at her needle and thread. "Such a waste of energy. What does it matter if you're wanted by others at all? You contribute. You work as hard as you can to help make this *haus* a home."

She nodded to herself, glancing down at the ever-growing pile of completed mending beside her for reassuring proof. It was true that she was a hard worker, and one who never complained, and she knew her parents appreciated that about her.

Unfortunately, it was also true that if she were never able to find a man who wanted to take her for his *fraa*, she would undoubtedly prove to be a burden as her parents moved into their golden years of age. They would have to continue to care for her long past the point when parents were meant to be relieved of that task. The mere thought of it was enough to make her shudder, and her eyes well up with tears.

"*Ach,* here you are!" Anna's *schweschder,* Ruth, exclaimed from the open screen door of the back porch. "I've been looking for you all over. I thought you had gone and disappeared."

"*Nee,* I've been right here the whole time," Anna protested, her heart hammering in her chest as she tried in vain to recover from her start. "And you frightened me half to death. You shouldn't sneak up on people like that, Ruth. You really shouldn't."

"I know," Ruth said with a dramatic sigh that wasn't quite able to make up for the glint of mischief shining in her cornflower eyes. "But sometimes, I just can't seem to help myself. And, anyway, I really was looking for you, and for what felt like the longest time. Have you been out here all day?"

"Why, I don't know," Anna answered with a small frown of confusion.

She looked out from beneath the porch's comfortably weathered ceiling and gazed up at the sky, trying to determine what time it was. Truth be told, she didn't have the first clue how long she had been out there on her own. That was one of the hazards of being a person who spent most of her waking hours on her own. Time had a way of losing itself, and sometimes, of disappearing altogether.

"Well, I think you have been," Ruth said decisively, her hands on her hips as she surveyed Anna's day's work with a scrutinizing eye. "And I think it's enough for today. It's time to put your work away, too."

"*Ach,* really?" Anna asked, laughing despite herself. "And what brought you to that conclusion?"

"My keen powers of observation," Ruth said, her expression kept serious for only a moment before she collapsed into a fit of giggles that Anna couldn't help but join in.

And that was the thing about Ruth, the thing that everybody who met her couldn't help but notice. Ruth was the sort of girl that people just wanted to be around, even if they couldn't quite put their finger on why. She was funny and kind, silly, and a little bit wild, and all of those things were absolutely contagious.

In short, Anna believed that her sweet, sixteen-year-old *schweschder* was all of the things that she herself was not. Whereas Anna was likely to blend seamlessly into the background of any gathering she was forced to attend, Ruth was always like a bright, shining star in a crowd.

Everyone wanted to be around her, and although she was still just a little bit too young to begin a courtship, it was already widely understood who she would eventually marry. It was understood with a confidence that Anna couldn't remember ever having about anything in her life.

Ruth and a boy named Jonathan Kemp had been thick as thieves for as long as anyone could remember, and their friendship seemed to be naturally evolving into something far deeper. While Jonathan was about to leave for his *Rumspringa,* people expected that when he returned to Faith's Creek, he and Ruth would begin courting. They would be wed, and Anna would officially be surpassed by her lovely younger *schweschder.*

"I'm serious, Anna," she whined now, reaching for Anna's hand and trying to tug her onto her feet. "It's time to put this away. Don't you want to have a little bit of adventure in your life?"

"What?" Anna asked with surprise and not a little bit of dread. "*Nee,* of course not. What are you going on about, anyhow?"

"Nothing," Ruth answered, a pretty pout on her pert, sixteen-year-old lips. "I'm just saying that it might not be such a bad thing for you to do something other than work and shut yourself away in the *haus*."

"It's a *wunderbaar haus*," Anna snapped back, her tone more severe than she intended, although she didn't seem to make it otherwise. "And I don't mind the work. I'm happy to do it. I'm happy to be useful to our parents. I think they need me to do what I do, anyhow. What would they think if I just ran off?"

"They would be pleased for you to have a little time to yourself," Ruth answered immediately, and with a confidence that Anna didn't think she had ever felt before in her life. "I was talking to *Mamm*..."

"About me?" Anna interrupted, finally getting to her feet as Ruth had wanted her to all along. "The two of you were talking about me without me being there?"

"*Jah*, but not anything bad," Ruth insisted, finally showing the faintest hint of uncertainty. "I was telling her that I wished the two of us spent more time together. Time outside of the *haus*, and she said she thought that was a lovely idea. She is the one who bade me come and find you. She told me you should come with me to game night."

That stopped Anna cold. The idea that two of the people she loved most in the world had come together to speak about the extent to which she was isolating herself made her feel exposed and ashamed. It was the very feeling she feared most, and so she kept herself apart as if it might keep her safe.

And yet, at the same time, there was a part of her that saw what Ruth was saying now as an opportunity. She saw it as a chance being offered to her, one that she was sorely tempted to take. Perhaps she wasn't destined to live out her days alone, after all, as unlikely as the possibility seemed. Maybe forcing herself to come out of her shell a little would offer her one of *Gott's* many blessings and rewards.

"*Jah,*" she said softly before she had time to convince herself not to speak at all.

"What?" Ruth asked, her eyes growing wide with disbelief. "What did you say?"

"I said *Jah,*" Anna repeated, smiling at her *schweschder's* obvious delight despite the butterflies fluttering wildly in her stomach. "All right. I'll accompany you into town tonight, just so long as you promise not to try and turn it into a habit."

Instead of answering, Ruth threw her arms around Anna's neck. Anna understood that Ruth's failure to agree to her terms meant that there would likely be similar requests in the future. At the moment, however, she found that she didn't really care. She was going to allow herself an adventure, and despite it being a small one, she was excited for what may come to pass.

Grab Amish Love in Faith's Creek a super value 15 Book Box Set now for FREE with Kindle Unlimited.

A Baby to Love

A Love Tested

Find all Sarah's books on Amazon and click the yellow follow button

This book is dedicated to the wonderful Amish people and the faithful life that they live.

Go in peace, my friends.

As an independent author, Sarah relies on your support. If you enjoyed this book, please leave a review on Amazon or Goodreads.

ABOUT THE AUTHOR

Sarah Miller was born in Pennsylvania and spent her childhood close to the Amish people. Weekends were spent doing chores; quilting or eventually babysitting in the community. She grew up to love their culture and the simple lifestyle and had many Amish friends. The one thing that you can guarantee when you are near the Amish, Sarah believes is that you will feel close to God.

Many years later she married Martin who is the love of her life and moved to England. There she started to write stories about the Amish. Recently after a lot of persuasion from her best friend she has decided to publish her stories. They draw on inspiration from her relationship with the Amish and with God and she hopes you enjoy reading them as much as she did writing them. Many of the stories are based on true events but names have been changed and even though they are authentic at times artistic license has been used.

Sarah likes her stories simple and to hold a message and they help bring her closer to her faith. She currently lives in Yorkshire, England with her husband Martin and seven very spoiled chickens.

She would love to meet you on Facebook at https://www.facebook.com/SarahMillerBooks

Sarah hopes her stories will both entertain and inspire and she wishes that you go with God.

www.ingramcontent.com/pod-product-compliance
Lightning Source LLC
Chambersburg PA
CBHW070831160726
48004CB00001B/338